THE BOOK OF DEVARAJ INDRA

arising out of use, inability to use, or about the reliability, accuracy or sufficiency of the information contained in this book.

DISCLAIMER

The purpose of this book is to provide entertainment or bring forward a fictional version of these mythological stories. No harm to anyone's sentiments and no disrespect to anyone's dignity is intended by the writer at all. Be it God, Human or any other species, this work is brought out with pure respect and humility. The tales were taken by Puranas and folklore, different versions were brought together and edited to showcase a fictional timeline. If due to any mistake, this offends anyone, I apologize very deeply.

Dedication

I wish I had the strength to write a prologue, epilogue and what not but this book wrote itself off and I followed, it from behind.

I grew up with these tales and legends, these are the gods I worship and their stories are sacred to me. The whole purpose of this piece was to collect my favorite ones and to string them together in a timeline.

Dedicating my art, skill, efforts or whatever I have within me to heavens above. If the gods ever read this book, I pray they don't dislike it

CONTENTS

The POV changes with characters clarified by the names of the chapters.

Purandara, Mahendra, Devendra, Devesha, Suresha, Shakra are all names of Devaraja Indra.

THE BOOK OF SHACHI

VAGRANT

BEGINNING

Tired of bringing storms to the world, he brought one into my life. He is without a sin, so pure to the world however in my eyes, he is my culprit. He is so perfect in every way of his existence that even an excellent critique like me cannot come up with an insult. How does he manage to do all that he does is forever a mystery to me. Sometimes I wonder about whatever I did to deserve having my fate tied to his. There are innumerable realms in existence, more worlds than mortals or non-mortals could ever count, and my husband owns them all. He rules the heaven and earth while keeping the underworld in check. He terrifies the residents of hell so much that I cannot help but disdain him.

If one could imagine a world gilded with gold as pure as manuka honey, a world that glimmers with sterling silver as white as the snowy caps of Himalayas then only perhaps one could imagine this world called *Devaloka*, the abode of the *devas*, the place wherein live the gods. This place which once was an enemy territory to me, is now where I belong. So uncomfortable it is to walk these gardens sometimes knowing I am going to remain an outsider. Have women ever owned a place of their own? The maiden house will treat you as a guest once you get married and the marital house will treat you as the 'addition' no matter how long you stay or how much you contribute.

Such is the destiny of my marriage- my maiden home no longer exists, I who has no family to return to, now live here in the shiny palaces where every wall is made of sapphires and rubies and every resident is born with virtues and characters exactly opposite to what I have been brought up with. I blame my beloved husband for this condition of mine. There was a me so young and so naive, a fawn trying to find her way and he came hunting like a wolf and I kept falling deeply in love with someone who I was told to never cross paths with.

The moment I was born, an entire realm of anti-gods rejoiced. I was the princess of the *Danavaloka*, the heir and dear daughter of the *Danava king Puloman*. My father, a great ruler of one of the strongest celestial races which always stood its ground against the *devas*; my great father, the king of *danavas* had worshipped *shakti* for too long. His ardent devotion to *shiva* and *shiva*'s eternal consort *shakti* was what got him blessed with a daughter- me.

My father who showered me with affection deeper than ocean, my lovely dear father who had never once allowed a moment of sadness to touch me, oh how foolishly did I betray him! I betrayed him when I took my vows of marriage with the one who destroyed all my father had. I was the one born with blood boiling hot enough to burn him and yet he was the one who melted my frozen with the warmth of his presence.

Was I wrong when I started worshipping him? Worshipping him in secret because I believed so dearly that he would save me from a fated mishappening that I always warned about, but little did I know that my saviour was that said mishappening and now I thank and curse my fate every day. I was *Poulomi,* the daughter of *Puloman,* the princess of *danavas*, an heir of hell.

But now I am **Indrani,** the queen consort to *Devaraja Indra*, the king of all gods, the ruler of heaven. And this is my story.

1.

Poulomi

The gods and anti-gods alike worshipped the supreme head, *Shiva.*

Shiva who never saw anyone as inferior or superior, and whose worship brought welfare to all. *Shiva* the one who engulfs entire existence itself, he who personifies ultimate death, *Shiva,* he who destroys was worshipped by all. The common link between *devas* and their rivalling forces, perhaps that is why he is *Mahadeva.*

I too was born in a family devoted to him, and like all the 'good' demons, I held my faith in *Shiva* but time and time again I found my refuge in *Vishnu.* He who is the sole force that kept everything in balance. *Vishnu* was more liked by *devas* since, he protected them and supported; or in simple words- the gods are only who they are because of *Narayan.*

Vishnu is the reason why *devas* had their power and authority over everything in the universe and *Vishnu* is also the reason why those who went against the *devas* always struggled. We are the *asuras,* the a-suras, the anti-suras which meant the anti-*devas* and hence *Vishnu* was mostly seen as a foe by our kind, but I was merely eight years of age when I developed this devotion to *Vishnu.* My *Sri-Hari Narayan,* whom I considered to be my brother.

My father lived a long life, a few million years which in realms like ours was normal. During his lifetime, he had many sons- my brothers but only one daughter- me. I never got along with my brothers. They thought differently, felt, and saw things differently and no matter how much I tried- I could not grow attached to them. There was only *Narayan* whom I considered close enough to share a sibling like affection with. Not a single day passed when I didn't worship him.

My family was never fond of my devotion to *Vishnu*, the only god we worship as ours is *Shiva* but rarely there are demons like who do go against the hellish restrictions. Perhaps it was my father's love for me or was it my *Guru Shukracharya*'s understanding for they allowed me to live and worship my way. They never agreed to my perspective of the world, but they respected it. I was never made to feel included, but no one ever made me feel left out either, at least not on purpose.

I lived a simple life, an amazingly simple life. To live inside this princess palace which I was never allowed to leave. Huge walls and hallways, guards at every door. No man other than family was ever allowed to enter this side of the royal premises. All that I ever grew up knowing in the name of the world outside, were my gardens. They huge enough to have woods and ponds but not enough to show me what a river or real jungle looked like. Any bird that was not a habitant of these trees was arrowed to death immediately if it ever flew in skies that I was told were my limits. My bed chambers, my vanity, my treasures- jewels, crowns and cloths, a small armoury of weapons I was trained to wield, a ballroom where I learnt to dance and sing, a few more rooms for amusement, windows, balconies, and another room attached to mine- a temple where I worshipped my *Vishnu*- alone because no other danava ever wanted to join in. This is what my world looked like. Vain, superficial, narrow and every day was suffocating.

I was a skilled warrior who was never allowed to participate in a war. I was the princess who was taught how to make a good queen, but I knew in my heart that no one would ever let me rule. I could sing, I could dance but I was told strictly by my mother to never showcase myself in front of a man. A princess was a title that came with truly little authority but with very heavy responsibilities. The only thing I was ever allowed to look- was dignified. Life was purposeless, it felt like a burden each passing dawn.

I was a little child who felt ridiculously trapped but as I grew into a young girl- the restrictions became tighter. I could not breathe. There were my maids and ladies in waiting- I had a few thousand of those but none were close enough to become my friends. You are the *danavi* princess- act like one. Cold, merciless, ambitious, and sharp- that's who we are- my mother would repeat such statements often enough till I learnt how to control my temperament completely.

I saw these maids everyday- they helped me get out of my bed and dressed me up- they picked everything so I would not have to carry any. I saw them talk to each other, sometimes they would laugh or sometimes they would cry but I was never allowed to join their conversations. The only time I was allowed to speak to my maids was when I had to pass demands and place my orders. I had the authority to berate, scold, beat and even execute any of these servant women- simply because I was their mistress, but I never yielded to such measures. I always hoped that if I was warm to my servants then maybe they too will provide some comfort in return but instead I was always the subject of their ridicule. I heard what they called me- the doomed princess.

Shiva had appeared to bless me the day I was born- my realm was honoured, our preceptor- *Shukracharya* was overwhelmed, my father was ecstatic. *Shiva* had said something along the lines of me being born as a form of Shakti and asked my father to let me go when the time arrives. I was too young to remember what exactly he told them, and no one ever gave me a clear answer when I asked them. This incident remained a taboo. All I knew was a prophecy was attached to my birth, it scared my kingdom, and some thought I was ominous. Father decided that day to keep me away from others, always under a watch- perhaps this is also one reason he didn't mind me devoting to *Vishnu* in the place of *Shiva*. They did not want *Mahadeva* to reveal the truth to me either.

I don't believe anyone in the *Danavaloka* had ever expected me to grow fond of *Vishnu* which happened eventually, and we were close enough to communicate intuitively. I saw him often in my dreams, he would talk through his idol, omens, signs, and miracles. *Vishnu* was the guiding force of my life, and the reason I felt safe were not the guards on duty, it was his protection, the strength that came through *Sri-Narayan*.

I had many teachers in my life, while others taught me scriptures, sciences, and arts. *Vishnu* taught me stories, tales of the forbidden, tales of the gods. It was through my dear *Narayan* that I learnt about *devas* and the *devaloka* where they lived. The *devas* when seen through the eyes of *Narayan* who graced them like a guardian and the *devas* when seen through the eyes of my family appeared as two different races, but they were the same.

Shukracharya has told me time and time again how the *devas*, the gods were not to be trusted under any circumstances. Even mentioning the name of one, got me scolded quite harshly by my mother, who wanted me to become nothing more than an obedient woman. My father told me that the only reason I should ever learn about the *devas* was to use this information against them, their destruction was our peace. The gods were a wretched race in the eyes of my people which is precisely why the conversations between me and my deity- *Vishnu* were a secret.

"I have turned sixteen of age today, are you not going to give me a present?" I asked *Vishnu*, as I sat in front of his idol, arranging flowers. My kingdom celebrated me coming of age and I sat in my temple all alone. "Do not taunt me like that *Poulomi*, you know well I am never empty handed for my devotees." The idol had responded. I intuitively got up to close the door and pull thick curtains over the windows. The temple filled with a bright golden light- and there came *Narayan*- the Sudarshan chakra in his upper right hand kept spinning with brilliance, the empty upper left hand in Abhaya mudra and the Koumodaki gada which his lower right hand held that appeared to be heavy but the lotus he held in his lower left arm was the prettiest thing in the world.

I rushed into his embrace- the only embrace which I found to be genuinely loving besides my that of. my parents. "You came, dear brother!" I exclaimed. "I had to." Said *Vishnu*, he continued as he asked- "What would you want as a present this year?" I thought for a moment, gathering my excited thoughts and spoke- "I just pray that you become my brother again in some other life, but in that life- our bond won't be a secret one- I hope you can protect me more openly and I promise I will care for you as a real sister." He laughed, elated I sensed, he nodded for a moment before turning to me and said- "If that is what you desire then very well-, but you shall wait till, I become Krishna again." What does that mean, I questioned him mentally, reading my thoughts he gestured- you will know when the time comes with his eyes.

"So, daughter of *Puloman*, what would you want for your birthday this year?" he had asked me the same question which he has been doing for the past eight years. That day, I felt grown, maybe more mature than I should have been. "Freedom" I replied.

"You wish to run away from the world, little one?" he inquired jokingly. "Nay, my lord. I wish to rule it." I answered. He smiled; he always does. He uttered- "Tathastu- so be it" as he blessed me with his hand. I had only said what I said thinking it was impossible, this was unexpected.

Bhagwan *Vishnu* had manifested an idol in his hands, it was man sitting on some animal which I hadn't seen before. The eyes of the man were blindfolded with a yellow cloth, and I looked up to his face inquisitively. "Who is this?" I asked and he handed over the idol to me. I couldn't make out what stone or metal it was. White, bright but lacked silvery colour. The touch of this idol had me feel sensations all over my body- I felt an impulse running through my nerves, my heart skipped a beat. "

Poulomi, this is *Devraja Indra*, the king of all *devas*, you asked for freedom, worship him- the tri*deva* had made him the king of all gods when he was a youth, he holds his power well. Worship him, he alone can fulfil all your desires. Freedom, power, whatever you wish for- just ask him, for you he would do anything."

"But- but I? My lord, my father says *Indra* is our worst enemy. I can't possibly worship him at home. They will lock me in my room forever." I hesitated. "Worship him in secret, there are tree groves and caves in the gardens you have raised. Who even visits those places besides you?" without saying any word further, *Vishnu* disappeared. All that was left was me with *Indra*'s idol in my hand and *Vishnu*'s idol in its usual place. I tried removing the blindfold, but it didn't come off. Giving up, I wrapped it in a shawl and left.

"I am off to visit my magnolia trees, they are in full bloom, and I strictly order to not be disturbed by anyone's company, no aides no maids." I commanded the guards as I went off to the most beautiful expansion of my tiny world. There was not a single flower or tree which I didn't love like a child of my own. My gardens were so well groomed even the residents of swarga would be jealous that is what everyone said when they came here. The magnolias were m*agni*ficent, enough trees in a circle to hide me completely, when these flowers will wither- the shade of other trees would be enough to cover. No one was allowed to enter my gardens without my permission, not even my dear father or my mother. I knew that the place which I had kept safe forever, will also keep me safe in return. There was a small dingy cave hidden by a curtain of hanging jasmines which I cleaned often. This would be the perfect spot to hide the idol, I thought.

A year passed; I was seventeen of age now. The blindfold of the idol never came off, I couldn't untie it and so I kept worshipping the eye-less god who I doubted had ever seen me. I was never sure whether the prayers which I uttered here in *danavaloka* would ever reach the heavens much above. *Indra*, did you ever know about my existence back then? My devotion to the one deity who had never answered my prayers or ever shown a sign of presence, kept growing more intense. Two more years passed, three more, five more, hundred more and eight hundred more. Eight hundred and eleven years, I dedicated to the idol worship of *Indra*, while the only god who ever responded was my *Vishnu*.

Our empire grew stronger and so did the walls between us and the *devas*. He never once sent a single omen; I was a mad woman who danced and wept in front of his idol knowing how blindfolded he was. Every time thought I went into the cave for my sadhana which I offered to *Shiva*, my family overjoyed that I was finally devoting time to *shiva* more than I worshipped *Vishnu*, would have had me thrown in the dungeons if they knew it was all for *Indra*, their worst nightmare.

I heard stories of *Indra* often in my father's court through the mouths of ministers and the gossips of my maids- they hated the sound of his very name, which I chanted whenever I was alone. He heard about his victory over the anti-gods, our Asuri clan was always distressed but I loved celebrating his valour more than mourning our defeat. I had asked him from freedom which I never received, it was the same *Poulomi* who danced in her chambers or played in her gardens, the only thing that changed were the veils I was forced to wear.

Always behind the curtains- you are a woman now, a virginal one- don't let men see you- you belong to your husband and your husband will be chosen by us- Oh *Poulomi*- the primary duty of a woman is to serve her husband and when we find a suitable one for you, only then shall a man ever get close enough to see your beauty. These words were repeated every now and then by my mother who told me to live inside curtains and cover my face even in front of the guards. I was so envious of my maids, so envious of every other woman I saw, they didn't have to follow these restraints.

I did however never veil in front of *Indra*; his eyes were already covered but more than that I wanted desperately to be seen by him. He will give me freedom, power, whatever I desire and that's all I believed. "Oh *Devendra*, liberate me just once, let me escape this hell just once and I will serve you in each lifetime of mine." I prayed on my knees, begging him to listen. I begged him every day, morning, noon, and night, I had fallen at his feet, asking to have a different life. A different life with freedom to be myself, to have enough power so I could live like my true self, but he never cared.

2.

Purandara

For the past eight hundred and eleven years, soon to become eight hundred and twelve years, this mysterious voice has been chanting my name. She started off as a sweet girl, childish perhaps adolescent but now has grown into a woman with refined speech. Morning, noon, and evening, three times, each day, she has been praying to me relentlessly and I have spent the past few centuries trying to find who she is.

I can always hear her chant, sing, and pray but whenever she spoke her name, there rang silence and nothing else. She talked to me every day but never about herself. She worships a blindfolded idol of mine that's all I knew about her. Wretched woman, stop begging me for mercy, how do you expect me to set you free when I can't even call your name the way you do mine.

You must live in some mysterious realm, one where my powers fell; I would've known you otherwise. All that you have ever asked for would have already been yours if you were close-by. Wretched woman, you make me go mad, I wake up and sleep to your voice. When you cry, I am not there to soothe you and that's the most helpless I have ever been. You sang to me last night; I was desperate to ask you why you were so happy.

You are as unreachable to me, as I am to you. Who taught you this way of worship, I feel like a waste of your devotion. It would've been better if you never held any faith in me but now you do, and I have lost myself to you. I beg you to not lose hope, I will find you someday. I too darling, pray to our fates so they would intertwine, I too would do anything to see you, to hear you, to heal you and feel you. Just for once, I wish to come across you and I swear upon my throne- I will do anything in my power to make your desires come true.

I have given you so many names just so I could call you mine. You are my honey, your voice is honey, all that you speak is honey, your weeping, your laugh- the only sweetness I crave is that of you, honey. My honey. I know you love flowers; you always bring them as an offering, I wonder whether you smell like one? I don't know that, and I don't care either, you are a flower to me, my favourite kind. Whatever you look or smell like, you are my little flower and what I wouldn't do to make you bloom forever! I am a king, I have a court to lead and the entire heaven to rule and look at me, lost in your thoughts the way a drop would lose itself in the ocean.

3.

Indrasabha I

The *devasabha*s at *Indraloka* aren't open for everyone to attend, celebrations occurred less often than they should because the courtiers are always preoccupied with some unavoidable tasks at hand. However, *Indrasabha*s are held regularly, the *devas* always attended to the agendas with a sense of duty while the minister and *guru* of *devas*, *Brihaspati* would be present listening to each of them and guiding where the gods failed.

Surya's famed *chari*ot which was forever drawn by a herd of seven horses had parked in front of *Indra*'s castle, the sound of which is enough to wake anyone up. *Devaguru Brihaspati* was the first to greet him within the court. "I see you are here today as well *Shani*, why though?" The aged *guru* questioned as he saw that following *Surya* was his toddler son. Not more than five years of age, the boy was clad in all-black clothes and walked in the shadow of his father just behind him.

The boy looked up to *Guru*'s face and replied after an intense moment of eye contact "I am here because I like court meetings and rajya*sabha*s. Father came too but you didn't ask him why." Even *Brihaspati* felt a bit intimidated by *Shani*'s gaze, something about those pitch-black eyes resembled black holes. "But your father *Surya deva* is a *deva*, a force of nature, a figure to be worshipped. It's his duty as a deity to attend these meetings." *Guru* answered breaking the eye contact and resuming to get seated on his designated chair, *Surya* as well found his place. The toddler ran off to a nearby window, shouting- "I am a *deva*putra, I am going to be a *deva* too. I belong in all the courts." *Surya* shook his head; *Shani* had summoned some baby crows to play with.

"Why can't you just stay at home and not meddle with adult affairs?" said another voice as the winds howled loudly. The curtains stirred in air, doors and windows trembled a few items fell on the ground. Out of thin air, manifested the figure of another divine man, *Vayu Deva* it was. *Shani* stuck out his tongue in childish rebellion. *Vayu* greeted *Brihaspati*, touched his *guru*'s feet, and got seated as well.

Surya flicked his fingers sending out sparks that erupted a fire in the middle of the court room, *Agni Deva* emerged from these very flames. "That's no way of summoning me, next time I am not showing up without a proper invocation." The fire god spoke trying to sound angry while all the others present just looked him up and down and nodded in a collective nod. Upset *Agni* found his chair. "I don't think anyone is obliged to invoke you; your job is to be present here." Snapped another presence, a standing vase had just shattered as the spilled water took the form of *Varuna Deva*.

Agni: Oh please! You should know-

Varuna: No please be quiet. You talk too much, and I am tired of it.

Agni: Don't start with me now. Sit somewhere far away from me.

Varuna: We always sit opposite to each other, you wouldn't burn if I came too close.

Agni: Speak for yourself, you would start fuming in a moment.

"Silence. My court is supposed to have a decorum." Said *Devaraja*, who finally entered through the main door. He looked around, ashes, broken articles, all things displaced. "I got that vase as a present from *Deva*-Vishwakarma just yesterday, you broke it in moment?" *Indra* always inquired but never waited for an answer, nonchalant all the time. He sighed and went straight to the dais where the highest of all thrones awaited.

"Let us now get straight to the agenda. *Devaguru*, kindly tell us why you summoned this *sabha*?" *Devendra* initiated, he slouched a little and rested his back against the *Indrasana*. He was tired, his attention was half present in the court and half lost in his thoughts, he gazes fixed on the floor, the others took notice of his disinterest. *Brihaspati* took his time articulating his words- "I have come to know that my rival *Shukracharya* is about to discover immortality, not only for himself but the entire clan of *asuras*." He released a breath and frowned, *Agni* gasped- "But other than Tri*deva* there is no other being who is immortalized, it's impossible to achieve, that's what you taught us."

Brihaspati glared at *Agni* for a moment and continued- "Well, *Shukra* the *acharya* of *Asuras* is proficient and wise. He is using his scholarly mind to 'research' some method that would practically making his kind into a race of immortal beings. Before you ask any further, no I don't know what exactly he is searching or making, but I know from my sources that his research is almost successful."

Varuna cried a bit, "But that's so unfair, we all here risk our lives almost every day fighting these demons and monsters and what not just to keep the cosmos in check and balance and they get to seek immortality. Why do we not seek it for ourselves instead? We are the old gods, the powers that maintain dharma."

The boy who was laying on the floor near *Surya*'s *asana* in the shadow casted by him peeked curiously upon hearing the word 'unfair.' *Shani* had now put down the baby crow he was playing with and ran quickly off to *Varuna*, hugging the elder one with his toddler hands to comfort him, he gently whispered- "That's fine, you will be all right. My father says you too have the secret of immortality deep within you. One day you might make our race immortal as well *Deva Varuna*. And *Shukracharya* is a great man."

Everyone raised they eyebrows, "*Surya*, why is your toddler calling your worst enemy a great man? And why does this toddler of godly lineage even aware about who *Shukra* is?" *Vayu* broke the silence with his question, the sorry sun god shook his head- "He is a curious child and a stubborn one, I can't hinder his exploration and growth now, can I?" *Vayu* nodded, "I see you are a poor father but a brilliant teacher, if I ever had a son, he would better behave but I will let you teach him." *Surya* visibly grew upset- "None of you here have wives or children except *Devaguru*, you all wouldn't get it."

"Oh, that is enough, if we are done providing emotional support to *Varuna* and parenting advise to *Surya*, can we come back to the topic of immortality?" This indirect approach is how *Brihaspati* scolded his students. *Indra* whose has kept his eyes closed till now shot awake and questioned with a sudden sense of urgency- "Did *Shukracharya* come up with this idea on his own? Who else is scheming with him?"

Devaguru who now only seemed proud and pleased with the input gave an unexpected reply- "*Danavaraja Puloman* is the man behind it. He champions and sponsors *Shukra* and but seeks for his clan of *Danavas* to be immortalized first."

Indra sighed loudly; *Agni* interjected- "Just how stubborn is *Puloman*? Haven't we defeated his army enough number of times?" *Shani* giggled a little, "Not more stubborn than me, right baba?" he looked up at *Surya* who signalled a yes and gestured the child to quiet down. "*Devaraja*? I like *Puloman*'s daughter too. *Poulomi* is a good girl." *Shani* added before he sat cross legged on the floor again. The courtiers of *Indrasabha* exchanged surprised glances, looking quizzically at each other and then towards the kid.

Agni was the first to ask, "*Puloman*, that demonic king has a daughter?" he was not the only one surprised. No one was aware about the *danavas* having a princess. Will she pose a threat to us? Is she dangerous and powerful like her father? Or just an ordinary woman.

Varuna who rarely shows any interest in the *sabha* seemed intrigued for once, "Never heard of any *Poulomi*, I thought *Puloman* had only sons." *Vayu* as always is the only adult concerned enough to make the right inquiry, "Again, *Shani*! Why do you know about *Puloman* or his daughter?"

"*Shukracharya*. I went to *Danavaloka* once with him." *Shani* said with his innocent tone, as intimidating of a kid he is, anyone can tell with ease when he is scared. The only thing he finds frightening is his father's anger. And unfortunately for him, *Surya* who is usually calm and composed, was in fact angry. "WHY? WHEN? YOU NEVER TOLD ME."

Shani has a habit of deliberately riling up *Surya*, he does it because in his childish brain this is the best method for grabbing his father's attention which he craves all the time. "I didn't feel like telling you. I am a big boy now. You don't get to control me."

Surya was containing himself; he went quiet for a moment trying to comprehend what his boy just said. *Shani* saw this as another opportunity, he continued with his childish innocence- "*Puloman* loves his daughter, but my father doesn't love me."

The only moment when you can catch *Suryadeva* being helpless is when he is dealing with *Shani*, and – "You are grounded for at least two months. No attending *devasabha*s either." These were the exact kinds of punishments that made *Shani* rebel more and more.

Indra who was quiet during the chatter almost cried- "Nay! Your child is genius. Now this is what I call intel. Prepare for a war just in case the hostage situation goes out of hand."

Vayu being the curious one, "Hostage situation?! You are not planning on to abducting that Princess *Poulomi*, are you?" *Indra* nodded more proudly than he should have. *Varuna* was first to interject, "I am out of this. Sounds nasty." Followed by *Agni*, "I am in on this. Sounds exciting."

Surya who has now calmed was pertinent with his inquiry, "*Devaguru*, you knew about *Puloman* having a daughter?"

Brihaspati seemed stern in his expression but sounded almost apologetic, "I know *Poulomi* well enough and take this command of mine seriously. No harming the princess, I do not condone dragging that poor girl in your plans."

Indra is to *Devaguru Brihaspati* what *Shani* is to *Suryadeva*, a difficult to manage stubborn child, "Do you know a better plan? Or do you wish for us to do nothing as *Shukracharya* figures out the formula of immortality. Besides, I am tired of *Puloman*!"

Shani who had resumed his play by now was appeasing to his father, "Am I still grounded?" "Yes, for three months now" *Surya* teased the boy, almost making him tear up.

Indra smiled, rarest phenomenon in *devaloka*, "No child, you can stay here at my place whenever you are bored of your father. And that's my decree as your king."

Shani's final response before resuming his play "… You are the best king and the best uncle I have!" Children are simple, you can play with yours or just abduct that of your enemies for personal advantage maybe this is what *Indra* concluded as he dismissed the court.

4.

Devaraj

"So, you will stay here for the night my boy?" *Surya* asked looking displeased. The other *devas* who had attended the *sabha* earlier had already left for their realms. *Surya* is always the first to come and the last to go but his toddler to whom he posed this question refused to budge. "I not going to punish you, let's just go home for today." He continued.

"NO. You said I was grounded so I am not leaving this place." *Shani* always answered his father in an angry tone, I wondered often and still do sometimes- is it because *Surya* is overly strict as a parent or overly lenient? Besides this boy has always been a stubborn and uncontrollable force so no one came in between the father son duo.

I heard *Surya deva* sigh for a moment, defeated he asked- "Very well, so how long will you stay here?" *Shani* glanced at my face for a moment, he had no intention of cooperating. I suggested- "Just let him be. I will take care of both your child and your concern. Besides, I must interrogate him."

"Fine, but remember your brother is waiting for you in *Suryaloka*. Come when you feel like playing with *Yama*." The elder one said as he boarded his *chari*ot. "Don't let him touch my toys till I come back." the boy warned as the *chari*ot pulled away.

Now I was left alone in the courtroom with my nephew who was more interested in playing with crows than engaging with me; doesn't matter I demand answers. *Puloman*, my archnemesis had a daughter but how come I wasn't aware? And why is the princess of *danavas* not a known figure? What is *Shukracharya* up to? Brahma, *Narayana*, *Mahadeva*, they are immortal, and it makes sense the cycle of creation, existence and destruction is immortal BUT can the beings who are merely a part of it be immortalized?

The boy came running to me, handing over a crow- "Play with me now, please?" Children are funny. "Tomorrow child, I have some urgent matter to attend to." He looked dejected for a moment- "Baba never has time for me." I glanced over at his frowning face but nah, my devotee is going to make her prayers soon, she always does. "Adults have work, *devas* just have too much of it. Play as much as you want while you still can, when you join us, you won't have time for anyone either."

"I will tell baba; you were trying to demoralize me" *Shani* speaks the language of warnings and judgements, precisely he is not easy to talk to. The only way you can threaten this kid is by mentioning his father- "Okay and I will tell my brother that his son was threatening me."

"Not fair, all this because of that woman, right?" I don't know who has the upper hand in this conversation anymore. "What woman?" Great, now my tone is bitter, and I am losing myself in her thoughts again. Yes, that woman.

"Your priestess or devotee or whoever she is." This child is hitting the sore spot again just how I long to know whoever she is. My flower, I miss her so much right now. "How do you know about her?" I asked, maybe I was wrong letting the kid stay for the night.

"I overhear Baba and other *devas* talking about you in *Suryaloka*." Oh, and that is not what I expected for an answer but makes sense. I probed further, "They do so often?" He stared at me intently before answering- "Oh! every time they meet, you are the topic of discussion." *Shani* is smiling, he knows he has the upper hand.

"Why does your baba allow you to stay during such meetings?" Just give me a normal answer for once. "Because he doesn't, I just have a lot of hiding spots." Yes, coming out of the mouth of *Shani*, this is practically normal.

"*Surya* should ground you more often." *Surya* is a family man and I wonder often how he manages his children. "Me being punished won't help you find that woman." And with this sentence, I was done for the day. My nights are lonely without her whoever she is, my pretty little flower. "Go to sleep now, I just want to hear her voice again." with this I somehow managed to tuck *Shani* in the bed and left for my room. My lonely room. Everything is going to remain lonely for me until I find you, honey. I pray to *Mahadeva* hoping to find you soon.

The next day wasn't particularly thrilling. *Devaguru Brihaspati* has left for his ashrama, he has some *yajnas* to perform. There were no meetings or any work to do besides *Agni* who had come to discuss the same matters as yesterday- *Puloman*. We both were trying to make *Shani* spill whatever he knew about *Danavaloka*.

"Why don't you have any toys here, *devaraja*?" the boy was sulking. "Because *Indra* doesn't have any children." *Agni* replied. "And why is that?" He answered again "He is not married yet." "Is marriage necessary to have children? Where do children come from?" Now we both were feeling awkward, I commended *Surya* for putting up with this every day.

"When two people love each other very…" I elbowed *Agni* to shut up. "It is not appropriate for you to know. Grow up and you will understand." Scolding children while respecting their dignity is difficult. "Devraja, would you marry that wretched woman of yours?" this question hit the nerves I didn't know of. "No, she is just someone who holds her faith in me." I lied, I never wanted to marry anyone ever but now I want her and no one else as my wife.

Shani looked sceptical, "Is she pretty?" caught off guard again, I am defenceless when the topic is her. "Maybe or maybe not, I have never had the fortune of seeing her." Realisations like this make me sad. It is not like I have never seen her, but I have seen her only in dreams, her face always blurred or veiled, I spent all my love on her in my dreams but the moment I wake up, she is just gone with all her memories.

"Hmm, she cannot be prettier than *Poulomi*." Aah, right this child brought me back to the actual woman I should be concerned about. "Is *Poulomi* pretty?" *Agni* posed the question; I thank him for holding the conversation in my stead.

"Yes, she is incredibly beautiful but not more than my maa." *Puloman* having an incredibly beautiful offspring is the incredible part. But to be fair, *Puloman* is not the worst looking man I know, for a danava, he seems handsome, tall, and muscular and intimidating. I have fought him many times and he is one of the most difficult opponents I have ever dealt with.

Agni kept the child engaged to figure out more information out of this tiny spy, "So how and where did you meet her?" *Shani*'s reply stunned me for a bit, "*Shivalaya, danavaloka.*"

"Elaborate" I had to command him. "I attended a *Shiva*-pujan at *Puloman*'s palace, *Shukracharya* was the priest." So, this child is that close with *Shukra*? *Surya* abhors the *acharya* of the *asuras* to his core. He is not going to be happy when he learns about this.

"Are the *Shiva* related pujas we do here in *devaloka* not enough for you, boy?" Yeah, now I am angry. I have devoted my life to *Mahadeva*, there is no other realm that can hold any religious gathering or ceremony better than us.

"Just admit that *Asuras* do it better." Snap, that's one of the worst sentences I have ever heard. "Agreed" *Agni* replied and I glared at him for a whole minute or two. The thing about my twin brother, *Agni deva* is that when you don't give him enough ghee for ahuti, he ends up pouring some in the fire of my rage.

We three continued to play for some time. *Shani* was dictatorial and we were happy being with a child and engaging in innocent pass times, I think often that if I did ever have children will they turn out like this too? What about my flower? Will she ever have children? Who would she have her children with? If I could, I would bless her a wonderful life with happy and healthy children. I wonder what kind of husband she will have though. Isn't she old enough to be married already besides how old is this *Poulomi*?

I lifted my brows and cued *Agni* to say something. He got the signal. "Hey kid? Is there a way we could meet *Poulomi*?" The toddler passed a few judgmental looks at us, for a tiniest bit, his eyes made me shudder. He yawned and told- "No. It would be next to impossible. *Poulomi* never leaves the royal palace of *danavaloka*, her baba is stricter than mine. She is rarely seen outside her chambers. She always covers her face, so not many recognise her."

"But there must be some way?" *Agni* interjected, *Shani* replied sarcastically- "Sure if you could deal with at least fifteen thousand skilled warriors that guard just her side of the palace and I have heard that a minimum to two or three thousand maids are always attending to her. Remember she is a princess of a realm only second to ours so there is no way *Puloman* will let you meet her. I have heard rumours of him executing men for even daring to speak of his daughter." That's frustrating, I muttered under my breath, but I shouldn't have expected anything less from the most powerful Asuri race.

The unfortunate part is that I can't take *Shani*'s words for it. As accurate as his observation maybe, he is still a kid who could be over or under stating the facts. "So, is there really no way of meeting her?" *Agni* has grown impatient, he always does.

"Why don't you join me when I go there the next time?" this baby is terrifying in the most innocent way, because "What do you mean by join you? Does *Surya* know you are planning to go again?" He made a hush hush sign with a finger on the lips- "If you tell baba on me then you lose your chance of meeting *Poulomi*." Again, I fear who he will become as a grown up, imagine this kid as a *deva* being worshipped. "I give up, we will join you. When are you going there?" Guess I will have to strategize with *Surya*'s child now, he is not going to be happy about this but ends justify the means. "Tomorrow"- he replied so tomorrow it is.

5.

Matrika

My throat is blasted. I am unable to speak at all and worse it had to happen today on *Shiva*-pujan, such an auspicious occasion and I am voiceless. Is it because of something I ate? Maybe I shouldn't have eaten the prasad that kid gave me. But how could I reject prasad? And he is just an innocent child. I suppose it's just a sore throat from singing too much yesterday.

I love these rare occasions so much; I finally get to leave the palace and see what my own kingdom looks like. *Danavaloka* is so peaceful and prosperous when the *devas* aren't at a war with us and how I wish this were always the case. So, I am sitting in my palanquin and only my regular maids are assisting me today, there aren't too many guards in my entourage today so maybe I can stop mid-way and explore some place.

Baba left earlier than usual, *Shukracharya* and others must be waiting for me as well. I wouldn't have been late had it not been for *Shani*. That troublesome kid, gave me a throat ache and is now sitting in front of me, how did he even convince my family to sit in my palanquin though? He might be the first godly blood trusted so much by *danavas* but *Acharya* is fond of him so we can't really question the child.

"*Poulomi*? Can you still not speak?" the boy turned his head up to stare at my face, he had even lifted my veil with his tiny hands, too comfortable. I had to nod, trying to utter the answer was pointless. "I am sorry, I didn't realize it would hurt you so much." The apology was genuine. This child despite having the blood of *devas* triggered by maternal instinct.

He continued playing in my lap, the palanquin moved slowly through the woods. In the core of this jungle was the *Shiva*laya which the folks of my realm cherished deeply. I am grateful to *Shani* for this delay, he made me sick just-right enough to be left behind and travel alone. I love my baba but the only thing I feel when he isn't around is freedom.

I massaged the boy's shoulders a little, a silent gesture, a plea. He looked up to me again, locking eyes which terrified me and understood just what I had to say. "STOP THE CARAVAN. *RAJAKUMARI POULOMI* IS FEELING UNWELL." He shouted while poking his head out the curtains. My palanquin was laid down, I finally got out. Aah the smell of sandalwood, I love these jungles so much, I wish I could visit often.

He commanded the servants again- "This is a forest, right? Go find herbs for the princess's throat and let her walk in the fresh air, she is experiencing motion sickness." This the kind of authority I crave which the child of *Surya* possessed naturally maybe that's why our *Acharya Shukra* lets him tag along. I drew the veil back, moved out of the palanquin and walked a little towards the trees, the maids and guards were being instructed by *Shani*, he is a handful to deal with. If he doesn't like you then he will put up the worse behaviour, I felt sorry for his mother quite often.

I heard a distinct call of some animal. Is it a bird's cry? Never heard such a sound before. I sense it is coming from that bush there. Do I call the guards? But I can't speak or call for anyone. Never mind this poor animal or bird seems to be in pain. Let me check on it, I will bring it to the *Shiva*laya, it will be fine.

Aah, just as I thought. It is a peacock, such majestic bird. But where did you come from? Exotic birds like peacocks don't exist here in *danavaloka*, the live amongst the *devas*. Did you fly here on your own? I wanted to ask but this bird and my throat both are injured. Maybe someone cruel had tortured it. Is this a prank? Who would do such a thing? Imagine leaving a bird all alone in a forest to die.

I kneeled near the peacock, trying to soothe its feathers. When I touched its body to check for any wounds, it straightened his neck, staring right at me; "Fatal mistake, princess." – said the peacock.

6.

Indrasabha II

The *devas* were seated in the court again, they awaited their king's arrival who had gone on some important mission which none knew what it really was. All attendees and courtiers were at ease except for *Surya*, who was furious. "I shouldn't have trusted them with my son." He huffed under his breath.

"We shouldn't have trusted your son either." *Agni*'s voice echoed as he manifested out of a torch nearby, engulfed with flames he held *Shani* in his arms, who unscathed seemed to be enjoying the 'upsies.' *Agni* walked handing over the kid to his father. "WHAT DID YOU DO THIS TIME?" *Surya* sounded defeated and angry at the once. *Shani* avoiding the direct eye contact buried his face in his father's chest softening the elder for a bit. "Sorry, I didn't mean to. I was angry, it happened because of my eyes again."

"His eyes, his gaze, he burnt an entire forest down in *danavaloka*. Lucky for him, fire is my element, so I brought him back. The *Shiva*laya could have been burnt too and I would have been guilty, I barely managed myself." *Agni* almost teared up, both him and *Shani* are experts at losing control over themselves when provoked maybe that's why *Shiva* matter so much to them. *Surya* feeling sorry for both chose to remain quiet.

"Where is *Indra*?" *Varuna* asked trying to shift the atmosphere. "In the air, I can sense him coming at a good speed." Answered *Vayu* who shot open all the windows, he was right. A peacock came flying like thunder and crashed on the floor like lightening. The *sabha* was startled, there lay a feminine figure beneath the bird, his claw was digging at her wrist.

While others were shocked and curious, the peacock changed his form. Coming out of his disguise there was *Indra* sitting in the middle of his court, holding the woman in his arms. He tried to shake her up, but she remained unconscious. His eyes were closed, her face was veiled. He seemed to be crying, *Varuna* came rushing to help- "Are you alright?"

"No" *Indra* nodded, "She poked my eyes so I knocked her unconscious, now I can't see, and she won't wake up." *Vayu* genuinely confused, "Okay and why are you still holding her? I will call some *Apsara or Gandharvini*." *Surya* agreed- "She is *kumari, a kanya*. It's not appropriate for you to touch her. Take her to some room."

"She blinded me in a flash, she is *Puloman*'s daughter. It's dangerous for others to go near her. Don't call anyone." *Indra* stood up holding the princess bridal style, "*Devasabha* is adjourned, all of you are dismissed for the day." "But your eyes?" a god asked to which, *Indra*'s reply was simple- "I am *Indra* the master of *Indris*, if one of my senses aren't working I still nine hundred and ninety-nine more to rely on."

7.

Shakra

I moved to the side barely dodging the knife attack, the blade sank deep into the mattress. Keeping her hostage in my bedroom wasn't a smart decision, I have a feeling she will destroy the place. "So, you can see now?" her anxiety is apparent in her anger. Being sarcastic while panicking, truly a *danavi*.

"Why are you surprised? Didn't your voice heal the same way my vision did?" I pinned her down on the bed, "Stop struggling, you will hurt yourself. I can't let you go before your father is exposed." Getting slapped by a demon princess was not what I expected. This is the first time someone has gotten close enough to do so and dang it hurts.

"Ouch" my hand reached for my cheek almost reflexively. She laughed, *Puloman*'s blood is – wait, this laugh! This voice, I have heard it before. The veil, could it be that? She tried pulling the knife back, I held her wrists tightly. Suddenly my desire to fight with her has vanished completely. "Who are you? And why are you after my father?" She demanded, that's the voice. Yes, she is the wretched woman. My flower is *Puloman*'s daughter or am I mistaken? "Your saviour." I said, hoping to test her.

"I have only one saviour and you are not him." This voice, this tone, this sharpness of tongue, all of this sounds like my woman. Is *Poulomi* my wretched woman? I am in disbelief, and presumably, she should be in too.

"Do you know who I am though?" Hostages are supposed to feel scared in unknown surroundings, she seems to be the scary one. Where does she even hide these many knives? "NO and I am not in-" Too much of protest in almost every word.

"I am *Devraja Indra* the worst nightmare of *Asuras*, especially your father." This silenced her for a moment, she gasped loud enough for me to confirm that yes, she is my honey. "Are you hurt?" I inquired as I relaxed my grip on her. "You are eight centuries late." I was waiting for you too, if only you knew.

"I will make up for it. Don't cry now please." We released each other and sat in silence for a moment. She rested her back against the headboard of the bed.

"All this time, I worshipped you with faith and your first act was to abduct me. What a waste of devotion." Sarcastic, cold, my favourite flower is a thorny one. "Nah honey, do you know how heartbroken I am? All this time I kept searching for that one woman who prayed for liberation daily and each time I fell for deeper, and it's you. My worst enemy's daughter."

"My, my, I am taken aback." Her speech is dramatic as always, I love that!

"So am I but that's the tr..." I am losing my train of thoughts being this close to her.

"My lord, never call me honey again." And here my heart skipped a beat, it always did whenever she called me that. "Stop calling me your lord then." I can hear that she is tearing up, my fault for forgetting how sensitive she can be. "But you are my lord, I have long before devoted my life to you." She has no reason to sound this sweet.

"And so, you are my honey, my flower. Not my fault that I never knew who you were or what your name was, so I gave you a few." Why did I tell her this? And why am I even blushing. But she giggled and so she won.

Her tone changed - "I have a name of my own, *Poulomi* is what the world calls me, daughter of *Puloman* it means." This is how she talks when she has a complaint.

"Darli- my jasmine, that name belongs to your father, its anything but your own. I would never call you *Poulomi*, I would rather just call you mine." I felt her stare, it sent a shiver down my spine.

"I have a name of my own, other than Poulomi. Only a few call me by that." She is sulking or at least I felt so.

"Then what is your real name?" I have never been curious about anything in life until today. "No" she denied, "My real name, go ask my father when the next time you face him."

"My flower has an incredible talent for making me feel helpless." Puloman wouldn't tell me her name unless he was dying.

"I don't like being called your flower."

"Sure, lotus."

"No!"

"Ah my jasmine, how many names will you reject?"

"How many do you have?"

"I gave you a different name for every time you chanted mine."

Finally, that quiet her down. "Why do you undermine my devotion for you?" Now that silenced me. "Nay honey, you underestimate mine. You are not the only devoted one."

The inky black night was lowering my power but evidently it increased hers. Is this how opposite we are really are? Only if the something other than the sun could shine at night.

My jasmine has gently swung her arms around me like a garland, "Why are you doing this to me?" It was a mistake grabbing her by the waist and now she was melting in my embrace or was it the other way around.

She made this bed feel relaxing for the first time, soft, warm, she is everything I need. "You are tired my lord, as inappropriate as it may seem, but I want you to rest." Stop it girl, you are my hostage, I abducted you. Don't be gentle with enemies, has *Puloman* not taught you that? I dragged her closer, held her tighter than I should have.

She pulled herself back. I know she is scared because me too. But if I lost my control, would hell break loose too? I am greedy for her touch, *Mahadeva*, please help me. Is this lust? But I am better than this. All of this is worse than wrong. And for once, I am willing to do the wrong.

This cannot be lust taking over me, I am *Indra* ever victorious over *indris*, no sense or sensation can overpower me except for my flower, she who smells like wet earth after rain and there she is all that I am thinking about. "I want to go back, if you are pleased by my worship then return me to father." She sobbed faintly. Don't trigger my emotions like that, you are just making this difficult. I have changed more in a day than I have ever in my life.

"NO. I abducted the princess, not my priestess that too for a purpose. You have served my idol for so long, why can't you serve your lord while he is sitting right in front you." I am reaching for her skin again; this is not who I am as a man.

Just leave me on your own, I have no will to let you go. "Serve you, how? All of this feels wrong." She is right about the wrong part. Disgusted by the question I asked- "You love me, don't you?"

"That's because you are my lord, my god. I worship you as my saviour." Please stop talking with such naivety.

"Do you love me or not?"

"Why are doing this to us?"

"US? What are we? Who am I to you? Who are you to me?"

"Us- One of us shouldn't be in this room."

"Will you run away if I leave?"

"I won't. You stole me, abducted from my realm. I am too dignified to just run back, swallow your pride, *Devendra*. Return me to my father, RESPECTFULLY." I laughed, I had to. I laughed for a good moment. I never would've returned her till *Puloman* had compromised anyway but now I am too selfish to let her go. Return? Never. Every bit and inch of her belongs in my palace, not her father's.

Scary how I am thinking this way. I shouldn't. Sinning. I am *Devaraj Indra*, why am I sinning for this woman? I left her alone quite apprehensively; the reluctance itself was embarrassing.

The next morning was chaotic, *Puloman* had arrived in my court which was unusual. I genuinely expected a son of his or some minister to come by but despite being the king, he is here himself. He loves my flower, a little too much doesn't he?

I am walking towards the throne room; flower is running to meet her father. The moment we entered, "Baba!" she screamed before almost jumping on him, I had to grab her arm and hold her back. In that moment all I received was the look of pure hatred from *Danavaraja*, having fought him a million times before, this is by far the scariest he has ever looked.

"You are hurting my daughter! If I see you touching her again, I am squashing your head with my bare hands, *INDRA*. Release her!" How rude.

Now I hate to admit that I didn't hold her back because she was taken as a hostage and that *Puloman* was the other party but because I got jealous. She didn't jump on me like that, my eyes were poked on the first meeting. This demonic king had only been away for a day and a night, I waited her arrival for centuries.

"Each time you have ever been against me, you have lost. Who are you threatening?" Despite the tension in the room my instinct was to hold my honey. I know well she shouldn't be in my arms, but my soul says hold on to her forever. *Puloman* has his face scrunched up; he is giving me the nastiest look he can.

"Can you have my daughter sent somewhere else. I will speak to you in private." Aah, my archnemesis is speaking my language. Wait, he will take her back? He is here to take my dear one with him. Suddenly this much anticipated meeting has turned sour. Too sour to bear.

"Flower, just go back to our room. I will come when I am done with your father." One thing that came to my notice is how I speak to her, as if she is a little child, my tone is always gentle with her. Even *Puloman* laughed, truly unexpected.

"Here my daughter, I brought this as a little present."- the idol, the blindfolded idol, my iconography. That is what my wretched woman worshipped? – "After you were taken and the forest burnt down, I had you searched everywhere. Found this your little secret in the same cave you lied about. We have a lot to talk about young lady."

My flower was scared, I could hear the heavy breathing through her veil, she is panicking, frantically nodding her head in a no gesture. "Baba, I- give me a minute" SOBBING. She is crying. That made me angry.

"You made her cry!" I accused. "*Poulomi*, please calm down. We will talk when all of this is over, give us a minute please. You are my brave daughter, aren't you?" *Puloman* treats her like she is no older than a six-year-old, maybe this is the reason she became so sensitive.

"Please honey, stop crying." My way of consoling- pull her in an embrace, luckily, she calmed but her father glared. Doesn't matter we both know our priority is this one woman.

After having her sent back, I occupied my throne on the dais, allowing *Puloman* to have a seat lower to mine. A gesture to show who has the upper hand, he refused to sit down. Too dignified? That might be the only reason I admire this monster.

8.

Puloman

"You shouldn't have touched my daughter like that." Trying to sound composed while thanking *Indra* on the inside, never saw this day coming.

"Apologize, I apologize but I cannot bear to watch her cry." He sounds like a boy in love, that is how I was with my wife back in my days of youth.

"Not that you fool! Why did you abduct her?" Only now was I realising the purpose of this meeting was diplomacy.

"You are sponsoring *Shukracharya* to find a method for immortality, aren't you? What am I supposed to do? Imagine you filthy *asuras* becoming imperishable." Arrogant, as always now this might be the only thing I admire in this warrior king, what a monster.

"You cannot stop *Shukracharya* by abducting my daughter, you foolish *deva*! *Shukra* is not being championed by us *Danavas* alone, the other races especially *Daityas,* they are the ones supporting him." *Indra* keeps getting distracted, he is not focused, that's odd.

"*Puloman*, do I look like I care about your Asuri alliance? If you want *Poulomi* back, then go ahead and tell me what exactly *Shukra* is doing." Frustrating, that's how any interaction with *Indra* would go, this boy frustrates me.

"I love nothing more than I love my daughter, but our *Acharya* is a wise man. Maybe he saw this coming." *Devendra* leaned forward; he has grown impatient. "Your point being?" he asked.

"I don't know exactly what *Acharya* is up to, neither am I aware of the objective nor of the procedure. We are just allied for our commonwealth of *asuras*, get it now *Suresha*?" He is not at my throat today, suspicious.

"So, if you cannot pass the information to me, that means I can keep your daughter here with me." That's his main objective? Disgusting

I sighed, "That shouldn't be your concern, *Devendra*! You are supposed to think of a different course of action to extract information about us." Why am I even schooling him?

"Ahan! You have waged so many wars against me, yet you could never defeat me, but *Poulomi*, well she conquered me a long time ago." He is back to his arrogant self- better.

"The only reason all you allied forces are alive is because I have been merciful. It wouldn't take me a moment to decapitate each and every one of you. Since you cannot give me the information or halt *Shukracharya*, I will keep your daughter here with me." Yes, *Devendra* seems to have lost his mind but then I found his shrine in my daughter's place.

I slumped on a chair nearby; he is too smitten by *Poulomi* to grasp the intensity of the situation. Relaxed and probably enjoying my predicament since he knows how restricted I feel.

"*Indra*, I wasn't here to take my daughter here in the first place. My request that you keep her safe here." Finally, I admitted my intent.

He looked at me with curious eyes, seems like he is more happy than surprised. "Why?" he asked pretending to sound serious, trying to hide his smile. I sense he is happy about my daughter's stay at his place, that eases me.

"The prince of *Daityas*, *Anuhlada* is the primary link of our alliance." I started with my explanation, keep speaking he gestured with his hands, "*Anuhlada* is no good of man, he is baloney. Always drunk with wine, lustful and disgusting. He is not a warrior in essence, but he is cruel. Brutal with enemies. He is the one who hates you more than I do and so he is the one protecting *Shukra*, not me. Keep *Poulomi* safe here, that's my request."

He is confused, I can sense it, but his face wouldn't show much of an expression. "I am keeping *Poulomi* here, but what has *Anuhlada* got anything to do with your request?" That was an expected question.

"*Anuhlada* lusts after her. He has been asking to marry *Poulomi* for a long time, I kept her safe all this time but now since the news of her abduction has spread, it will trigger his impulses."

Devendra was horrified, his face was filled with disdain. "And you fear that if a war breaks out and you are defeated then *Anuhlada* would capture *Poulomi*." Aah, finally he understands.

"Keep *Poulomi* here, *Anuhlada* wouldn't attack you easily, but I know he is coming after me soon. If I win this war, I will ask *Shukracharya* to stop on our behalf and my daughter will be returned to danavaloka. But in case I lose, you know exactly what to do." Request, this was a request.

Indra stood up, he seems to be thinking about a lot of things at once, "Oh! I know exactly what to do. By fate if you don't get the opportunity to skin Anuhlada alive and slay his body in a million pieces, then I will. Either way, he is not coming anywhere near my *Poulomi*."

I shouldn't have laughed but I did, this is my first time seeing him act so boyish, "Don't laugh at me." He said, "You act around *Poulomi*, the way I did around her mother. Keep her safe and pure till I return, I trust you wouldn't outrage her modesty."

My worst enemy, but there is no one I trust more than you when it comes to my daughter.

"What is her real name?" he asked as I turned my back to exit this place. "If by Shiva's will, one of us was dying on a battlefield only then you would know." Answering so, I walked out.

9.

Mahendra

It has been a few weeks since my meeting with *Puloman*, my lovely flower has been staying in the *Ranivaas* of *Indraloka*. The palace has started adapting to her place, the gardens are her favourite even here, the peacocks, the rabbits all animals are enticed by her sweetness.

Even *Airavat* my beloved mount and best friend has grown closer to her. But can I blame him? She is simply perfect in every sense.

I have tried respecting her dignity and her fer father's request. I avoid touching or going too near her, all I do is admire her from afar. She veils all the time, just once I want to see her face. Her vastra cover all parts of her body, from shoulders to ankles, she is hidden in modesty.

So graceful, so pure, so innocent but her curves betray her attempts of modesty. Or maybe its just my eyes, I stare at her all the time, trying to imagine what she looks like under all that fabric. How would it feel to hold her in my arms? Is her skin soft like feathers or light like the clouds? Her innocence is making me grow wild each day.

She and I know both know that *Puloman* is now at war with *Anuhlada*, and I don't know which side to support. If *Puloman* wins then he will demand his daughter back. But I don't want him to lose to that daitya, *Anuhlada*, though we have never met, I hope to rip you apart just for thinking about my flower.

My innocent lamb is swinging in the garden, this is my opportunity to go and sit with her. She smells of wet earth when it rains, but I am the rain. Her fragrance is the proof of how much she belongs to me. Should anyone ever think about separating us, wouldn't I go mad?

"My lord, why are you here? Do you not have the *sabha* today?" She knows my routine by now, I know hers. I am busy with *devasabha*s and occasional battles, she finds her peace in these gardens or playing around in *Ranivaas*.

I should have held her captive in my room, could've come up with an excuse to why it is not safe for me to leave her alone. Why was I foolish enough to let her own the palace? That too a particular part of the castle which would have belonged to my future wife.

Ranivaas, the queen's residency is a place no woman has ever stayed in, but my flower has left her impression there, her fragrance mingles with bedsheets there and this is low of me to go there when she is not present, I lie on the same bed she sleeps on, just a very indirect way of expressing her.

"Stop calling me lord, chant my name the way you used to." She giggled, she does so often. Giggling, dancing, singing, and playing with children or animals that is all she does here, and she makes me feel alive in a way I never did before.

Puloman doesn't deserve to have her, *Anuhlada* doesn't deserve her, no other *deva* or sage is fit to be with her, but do I deserve her? Even if I don't, I am far too gone and selfish. I will kill and die before I ever let her go.

"*Devendra*, why are you here right now? Have you no other matters to attend?" Only she has the authority to inquire about my whereabouts, who else would dare ask "why" to the king of gods?

"The *devas* are all busy with their work today. Do you mind me being with you? I asked shyly, she nodded- "No, why would I?" she said, placing her head on my shoulder, never before have I sat on this swing. I didn't know there was a swing in this garden, to be honest I never realised there was a garden like this in *Indraloka*.

"*Amravati*" she muttered, I hummed, "This garden is my favourite place in *Indraloka*, I name it *Amravati*." I chuckled, so now she is naming places in my realm, wonder why I am never did?

"I feel lonely when you get busy with your work, what exactly is your work." She has relaxed more; I can feel her soft tiny palms massaging my bicep gently. I am blushing for the first time in my life, is she really that innocent or is she aware of the affect she has on me?

"I know you have never been to your father's court, why don't you come and attend the *devasabha* tomorrow?" I made the offer thinking maybe if she were by my side, I wouldn't be distracted by her thoughts.

10.

Mahendri

Why did I wake up with the feeling of deep loss? My gut tells that I have lost something very dear to me. It took only a moment to put on my shringaar and I was walked half-heartedly to the *sabha*.

My veil is irritating me today, but I can see the *sabha* is in chaos. *Shani* and his elder brother *Yama* were the first to come running towards me, "My baba will protect your baba, don't worry too much." This is the first sentence I hear! What does it even mean?

Indra and others are wearing their kavach, armours and kavach are all I can see here. *Devendra* walked towards me, we embraced each other instinctively. "Flower" he whispered softly.

I looked up to his face in horror, he held me too firmly, "*Daityas* and *Danavas* will now be at a war with us *Devas*." He declared and I was left dumbfounded. Why I muttered with a cry.

"I received a message from *Puloman*, *Shukracharya* has gone missing nowhere to be found. *Anuhlada* has almost won over your kingdom. It is a matter of hours till your clan is defeated because some important minister has betrayed your father. The *daityas* have officially declared an attack on us too." The warmth of his body helped me recover from the shock.

"My father is a warrior, so am I. This was expected." I said as I touched his armour. *Indra* held my hand, touching it with his lips. This was more unexpected than the news itself, the other *devas* and even the devis who were present were staring at us.

He lifted me up in his arms, walking towards his throne, he sat me down where he should be sitting. I don't remember what happened to us both in the moment, my fears vanished, I didn't cry anymore. He took off his crown, the mukut of *devaraja* and place it on my head.

"Rule the heavens while I am gone." He said that so easily, I was a princess who never left her palace but this man, *Devaraja Indra* is asking his enemy's daughter to rule his kingdom.

I was not left with much choice but to slice my thumb a little, my blood became his tilak. "Glories to you *Devendra*, may you forever be victorious." He smiled; he knows I used to add these words in my prayers.

Agni and *Vayu* remained in *Devaloka* as the guardians and protectors. *Indra* left for the battlefield. His army was the most skilled, *Aryaman*, *Surya*, *Vayu*, and many other *devas* had joined him. *Surya*'s wife, devi *Sanjana* took all the children with her to somewhere safer.

Devaguru Brihaspati and I remained alone in *Indra*'s throne room, "GOVERN." He said, run the world same way as *Devendra* does. There wasn't a hint of mockery in his tone, just confidence. I pray to *Sri Hari Vishnu* to keep him safe.

Days passed, each being more dreadful than the previous one. I didn't receive of any news from the battlefield until today. *Devaguru* has informed me that the *devas* have emerged victorious.

I was sitting on the *Indrasana* when I saw the entourage of heroes come home. *Indra* came in, throwing the severed head of *Anuhlada* on the floor, the others followed behind him. He walked up the dais, kneeling in front of me.

I sat next to him, letting him hold me. "I am sorry, I couldn't save him." He whispered. I knew what it meant. My nails dug deep into his flesh; I cried in his arms. Baba was no more, *Anuhlada* had killed him before he died at the hands of *Indra*.

"Don't be sorry, my lord. My father, a warrior, died on the battlefield. I am honoured to be his daughter. Thank you for avenging him." I said, tracing his jaw with my fingers.

Devaguru cleared his throat, I felt interrupted till I realise the others felt awkward watching us. We got up and I noticed what the soldiers have brought with them.

An empty palanquin, it was my palanquin that I used back in *danavaloka*. *Indra* asked *Agni* to step forward. The fire god, held in his hand, a plate of gold, a set of bridal dress, a bowl of turmeric and a coconut, most importantly there was a small box of sindoor. "Your baba gave your hand in marriage before passing away. Shachi, will you be my wife?"

THE BOOK OF SURYAPUTRAS

11.

Shani

I remember being a child sitting close to my father's asana in the devasabha, Suryadeva worked the hardest, he used to be the most diligent of all devas when it came to work, always too punctual but what did he ever get in return? His asana was placed at the last ends, near the exits much far away from other devas and so I always sat near him to keep him company.

It wasn't that the devas hated or disrespected him, just that the tapa and teja of Surya, the heat of the sun was unbearable to almost everyone including Indra. Even my siblings, Yama, Yami and Tapti would avoid coming close to our father.

My mother was the only one had never complained about his tapa and neither did I. In all honesty, I craved my father's light the most. I had a habit of following him everywhere, ever since I was born al I ever did was trail my father, Surya just as a shadow would. His shadow, the shadow of the sun was my comfort, my safe space. I loved the darkness that his light gave birth too.

Perhaps it was my habit of always staying near him or maybe him trying his best to not burn me, but I never found my father's heat to be unbearable. I craved his warmth; it nourished the way a child is nourished with breastmilk. My mother Sanjana was always busy taking care of us all, she treated each child of hers with equal love and adoration, but father favoured his daughters Yamuna and Tapti over me and Yama.

Yama couldn't care less about his validation, he was popular, really popular among everyone in Swarga. He was the most handsome, dashing, charming and intelligent. He was the better behaved one between us and so he was well liked but I followed my fathers in ways that were out of my control.

My father's heat and my own gaze, no one ever dared come near it. Whatever I saw burnt the same way my father's touch would burn it. Well, Pitashree brought fire but my eyes they brought bad luck. Even though me and my baba were invited everywhere, we were not welcome.

I remember when Yama and I had started handling the work in Suryaloka, my father who was born with the ability to heal almost any ability was not capable of healing himself. Baba like every other star in the galaxy had started to burn himself out. He was told to stop attending Devasabhas, just make the sunrise and sunset at places and rest at home, even Surya himself was unable to bear his heat. He used to be in pain, he suffered because of his own power every day.

Every day I woke up trying to achieve something that would make my father proud, but his love was never enough for me. Surya was never the type to show affection, perhaps that's why I kept craving his proximity more as time passed. I had no real purpose yet, I was a devaputra not a deva, my only duty which I understood was to find ways to make my father feel good about having me as his son. I wanted to become my father's favourite.

But all me and my baba did were arguments, there wasn't a single conversation we had which didn't end as a debate, sad part is neither of us would accept losing to the other one. Father brought light to darkness, knowledge to ignorance, I was convinced he was wiser than Devendra ever could be and so arguing with my father was the only lesson I attended. I didn't care much about Guru Brihaspati or Acharya Shukra had to say about a subject, as long as my father would debate with me on it, that's what mattered to me.

Father knew this and so he never stopped me from anything. "Your child is so disrespectful to you, Suryadeva, teach him better." "Surya why don't you punish Shani often?" "How did he turn out to be so different than Yama?" I heard them all say such things to my father all the time.

My pitashree, yes, I called him Pitashree when we were alone that's how I showed my respect to him. My pitashree would pretend to be the strict and harsh parent in front of others, I too would put a show for this audience, Suryadeva, I called him in public so others would show him respect too.

But when alone my Pitashree was a gentle and calm man, all he ever did was take care of others and answer every question of mine despite of how childish they were. The world was a rough place, I was judged by everyone mercilessly only my Pitashree showed me what a good balance of grace, forgiveness and punishment looked like. The non-judgemental attitude of my father towards me and the fair judgement he showcased to the world; all of this inspired me to follow the path of justice.

Anyone who knew me or my father, thought I hated him, but he has always been my greatest inspiration, I like it, I like to keep our bond a secret.

I was sitting in my father's room, he was laying on the bed, even the sheets would have burnt had they not been constructed by Vishwakarma. Pitashree was weak, he had grown weaker with all his powers exhausting him, he was burning, and I feared dying because of the heat.

Dear death, O Mahakaal, take anyone but my father. I prayed to Shiva daily, this same sentence repeated in my head all the time.

Varuna deva had entered, he still had some resistance to the heat. He came to take away the excessive tapa of my father. "What do you with this? I can consume the teja of Surya, he is my father, I can take care of him then why are you stealing his teja, it belongs to me!" I cried; I know I sound ridiculous to him. This wasn't the first time; Varuna had been helping my father by consuming some of the sun's heat.

"You do realise there is someone who lives in the ocean, he is cold, very cold. He craves your fathers heat and light more than you ever will, let him feed on this teja please." Varuna said as he was almost about to leave the room, Yama entered.

He reeked of heavy perfume, Yama was in flashy garments again, he was definitely at some Utsav or attending a celebration again.

"How is Sri Hari? Did you get me the permission to meet him? When can I meet Narayan again?" He was already bombarding the poor water god with his questions. Yama had developed a few hobbies, reading scriptures, going out with apsaras, visiting the ashrama of our grandfather and asking other devas about Sri Vishnu. He was obsessed with Narayan, but I couldn't blame him, I had the same obsession with Shiva.

Varuna deva visited our realm often, both him and my father Surya were aspects of Narayan, Yama took the Narayan part too seriously, this was his third time in the month where he was practically begging Varuna to visit Ksheer Sagar.

12.

Surya

I had woken up feeling cooler than before, either some of my teja was taken away by Varuna or Shani had been consuming my heat again. He was born with a dark blue complexion of the sky, resembling Vishnu to some extent but now Shani was tanned, his skin is turning charcoal black, I have told him to stop taking my heat, it is harming him, but that boy never listens.

I walked to the window, there my boys were having a gada-dhwandh, sparring with a mace again, they don't realise how much they truly grown. I remember well Yama being full of energy and Shani being full of anger, had been chewing my ears off to learn martial arts and combat.

Sri Narayan held his Koumodaki all the time, my gada was replica of his. I had to gift a gada, to each of my boys. They did everything together, learning, sparring, playing, it was hard to tell which brother was copying the other one. Not giving both of them the same treatment would result in week or even month-long tantrums.

I find it so heavy, walking towards them. These grounds of Suryaloka are where I first taught them how to use their gadas, this is where I taught them wrestling and even gave them the access to

Suryastra, now I know for certain they would defeat me easily in a fight. Grown too much, Shani used to crawl everywhere behind me and now he walks ahead of me, trying to handle my work. Yama, I would kneel to hug that little boy and now he reached my shoulders. Their 'Baba' became Pitashree in the blink of an eye. They went from being Balak Shani and Balak Yama to the Kumaras of Suryaloka. I can hear their murmur clearly.

"Pitamaha Kashyap was asking about you again. He says you should put more attention to your studies." Yama was trying to scold his brother, who in return said something surprising.

"Rishi Kashyap doesn't know your attention was caught by Dhumorna." Shani was in a playful mood, a rarity. I wonder who Dhumorna is.

"Aah, her. Dhumorna, be respectful to her Shani, she will be your sister-in-law when I marry her." Yama sound dreamy.

"Really? She has rejected your proposal more than three times, all because you roam around with a new woman every day." Shani teased.

"She will fall for me some day, every woman does. I may have my fun time with others, but her I will make my wife when she agrees. How is Dhamini?" Yama returned the taunts.

"She is pretty. If only my eyes didn't destroy almost everything they glance at, I would stare at her all the time. I- but don't bring her in between." This is the first time in my life when I heard Shani being shy, even though he is dark in complexion, I can see his blush.

"So, you see brother, we do everything together. How about we get married on the same day?" Yama has started fantasizing about his wedding already, just how much have the boys really grown?

"Sure! Who will talk to father though? I am never talking to Suryadeva about the girl I like." Shani has this old habit of turning every fun conversation into a dead serious one. The boys giggled, adorable.

"And why not? I will have a say whenever you both get married, that's my right as your father." I finally intervened; the brothers were surprised.

Days passed; Shani remained by my side. He often complaint about his eyes and I felt sorry, his powers were genetic. My teja and tapa manifested in him very differently compared to any other child of mine. Yama was busy being a socialite. Until one day, Indra came by.

"You know the new planet Earth? A mortal realm? Brahma plans to create something called Manyshya-jati, human life down there. My order is that you send your children down there to test the habitability. Don't send Shani though, he will destroy Earth in a moment." Devendra came to us devas personally only when he had the most ridiculous requests, his pride knows no bound.

Having no option, Yama and Yami, my first set of twins have gone to Earth, bhoolok. Yamuna took the form of river and flowed there endlessly, her waters brought greenery and prosperity, she brought life to the animals. My favourite child, my lovely daughter. Yama lived there as man.

Until one fateful day Devendra arrived in Suryaloka again, almost every other deva followed him. Yami walked along with them, crying, she went straight to her mother hugging her. I stood there dumbfounded when I saw what they had with them, my son's dead body.

Devaputra Kumar Yama, Suryaputra Yama was lying there dead, on the arthi. My father Kashyap have arrived, he didn't lose his son, I did.

I dropped to my knees, his face, his once beautiful face which I couldn't see anymore as tears blurred my vision. I hugged his body, his lifeless body couldn't sustain my heat, it burnt a little and I backed off. No, not this way, I cannot burn my own son. My dear child.

"What is this? Why is there a crowd?" Shani had a habit of waking up late, this noon was a morning to him. He came running straight not expecting to see what he did.

He pushed me off, he was angry. He was furious, he held Yama close to his chest. Even when lifeless, Yama's body seemed to be embracing Shani. Who did this to you? You are lying right?

"Baba, Yama is only pretending to be dead right? This is a joke, right? Why are you pulling off such a cruel prank?" His voice was heavy, he will never move on from this. I won't either but I am too absent to process.

"It happened at night, all of a sudden. We suspect the asuras might have." Indra tried speaking but Shani had punched him across the face, this time I won't stop him. Shani be as stubborn as you like today, I allow you to disrespect, to fight and rebel. Both you and I lost a dear one.

"DEVRAJA INDRA, MY BROTHER. YOU KILLED HIM. WE DON'T HAVE MRIT SANJEEVANI, THE ASURAS DO AND YET YOU SENT MY BROTHER ALONE ON EARTH." Shani roared, "I will kill each and every deva today first, then the asuras." His eyes were fuming black, I cannot stop him.

"Shani, please! Kill us all you want but let me cremate your brother first." Agni was so cruel with his words, how can I? Why not me? My heat was killing me already.

"No, stay away. I WILL BURN THE DEVALOK!" Shani screamed, he picked up Yama's body and ran off to his to crow. He was flying away, disappearing, I had nothing left in me. I don't remember who summoned my chariot, but I followed behind Shani. The others did too.

We arrived at Kailash, the abode of Shiva. "MAHADEVA! SHOW YOURSELF NOW, I INVOKE YOU." Shani screamed; he was too reluctant to let go of Yama's body which had started to decay. Losing one son is enough pain, don't make me lose you too, Shani! There was so much I wanted to say, to screech, to shout but my voice abandoned me.

With messy dreadlocks and Ganga on his head, a body smeared in ashes of the dead. Would this Shiva smear my son's ashes on himself too? I cannot fathom, I feel I am dying too.

There stood Shiva, in front of Shani. I stood at a distance; I had no strength to walk up to them. "Mahadeva, like a mad dog I worshipped you every day. Ever since I was conceived in my mother's womb, you are all I prayed to. I prayed every day for my sick father who heals the world. I told you to take anyone but him and you snatched my brother?" Shani scared everyone; he looked like he would have attacked Shiva.

"How dare you? Nothing is dearer to me than Yama, you either give him back to me or else I will follow him to wherever he has gone to." Shani has broken down completely.

"NO!" I screamed, I prayed silently, don't take another son of mine. Shiva smiled. Salt in the wound? The god of kala was laughing at my loss or something I didn't understand.

Yama moved, his hands. He moved enough to embrace Shani. "Don't follow me you idiot, I came back for you." He laughed. Yama was talking. He groaned in pain and Shani dropped him down on the snowy grounds. Shani was also quick to kick his brother, "Is this a joke? Who does that? I will kill you for real this time!" Justified anger, I was relieved. Yama got up laughing, "No I was dead all this time, hearing and watching all of you as a soul then great Shiva brought me back to life." He said.

Shiva who was silent till now, spoke- "Yama was the first ever being to ever die on the mortal realm of earth, he was the first ever being to witness Pitruloka, he alone now has become the ancestor to all the beings who shall ever inherit the earth which from now on, shall also be known as Mrityuloka."

I bowed, the other devas who only now felt courageous enough to come close, also kneeled in front of him. In a span of few hours, I had witnessed the death and revival of my son.

"Yama, you are the first deva to experience death. This fate I wrote for you, from now on you shall become the god of death itself, you shall be the devta of mrityu. Not only will make the souls cross over, but you alone are also the authority to decide which soul goes to heaven, hell or other realm. Yama, you alone shall decide where the next incarnation of any humans shall take place. Here take this Paash which when thrown by you, shall extract the soul from the body. This is Yamapaash."

Shiva had just made my son the god of the death as he handed over a noose to him. Yama, you foolish boy are laughing so carelessly after ripping my heart apart! Oh, how grateful I am to have my child well and alive. Or maybe he is dead?

"Both!" Yama mouthed looking at me, "I am both eternally alive and dead forever at once." He declared, as he engaged in a playful fistfight with his brother.

13.

Shani

Ever since my brother found his purpose of moving the dead and ruling the underworld, he has been busy with his work.

Father is still growing in his powers and with his heat, his anger has increased too. Surya deva switch from the calm man he is, to highly short tempered within moments, which is why talking to him has always ended in an argument.

I used to enjoy our debates, but Yama is not there to take my side anymore, with no one mediating between us, the fights between me and my 'pitashree' have become distasteful.

I have told my father many times before that I have zero interest in becoming a disciple of Brihaspati, his perspective is different, and he should keep Devendra in check anyway. I prefer Shukra but father despises him.

Yama has become even more of socialite, not only the women in swarga but even the mortals of earth have started being infatuated by his beauty. I agree my brother has handsome most features, but he has been slacking off so much that I have to keep a track of karma, good and bad deeds because he delegated his work to me. So annoying.

"Shani, SHANI! Look what happened." I heard him scream, more work. What's next, me procuring souls out of body instead of him? "Shani! Get down in here, this is urgent." I sighed as I started walking towards the palace halls but was surprised to see a monstrous figure in the corridors.

An Asura? Why is he in Suryaloka? How hideous and intimidating he is. I have seen better looking Rakshasas before, his horns are scary.

"Who are you? What is a strange looking creature doing here in Suryaloka?" I asked in a rough tone, not knowing whether he was invited or invading the space.

"Oh, foolish boy! It's me, Yama!" The monster is trying to impersonate my brother, great now I have to finish him off.

"No need to take that gada out, and don't call anyone. It really is me, your brother. I told you to note down the karma of some people in the morning, didn't I?" The monster said something only Yama would know, I eased and went in close. By the way he pulled me in a hug and punched my back, yes that is definitely my brother.

"What happened? I am going to kill whoever did this to your face!" Wiping the tears away from my brother's face, never thought this day would come. He is the elder one.

"SHIVA! Shiva did this to me." He broke down completely and I was silenced for a good moment. I took him back to the room before anyone hears the commotion.

"No one is going to believe you." I uttered. "I know." He nodded before explaining the situation, this whole mess seems like his fault.

Apparently, Yama was supposed to visit Pitruloka and judge the dead souls, the same souls whose karma I was keeping a track of. He literally delegated half his work and still my brother thought it is a clever idea to attend a gathering instead.

"So, all I ever did was dance with some women and those apsaras like me too! They invited me but then Shiva called me because I wasn't fulfilling my duties. He then ordered me to bring him some water from a nearby lake but when I saw the reflection in the water. THIS! I HAD TURNED INTO THIS TERRIBLE MONSTER!"

Yama cried, I sighed. What a day! If father ever gets to know that he was making me do the work, indulging in luxury and angered Shiva enough to be cursed then Yama will be in a greater trouble, our father is extremely strict when it comes to kartavya and naitikta.

I told him- "Run before baba sees you! He a lives by his ideals of karma and dharma and will disown you for this debauchery!"

"I cannot live like this" he sobbed, "These horns are terrible…I look like a monster… I had toned muscles, this is an ugly belly!" he kept sobbing, "My face was sharp like our mother but now I have this unkempt moustache and beard like you and baba!" Shiva cursed him right, what does that even mean?

"AM I AND BABA UGLY FOR HAVING A MOUSTACHE? THAT'S MANHOOD!" great, I am angrier than ever. Mahadeva didn't curse Yama due to his negligence, he did it because my brother has become so full of himself. Being so obsessed with one's physical appearance that you act with arrogance, this serves Yama right.

But I cannot abandon my brother, he is the other half of me- "Leave before Pitashree comes back, just leave Suryaloka. Go atone, make penance for Sri Hari and worship Narayan."

Sri Hari will have mercy on him, he is devoted to Narayan and so is our father. "But where do I go?" He asked, calming down a little.

"PITRULOKA! Just leave, I will tell baba you felt a call for devotion."

 "But the work?"

"I am good at making events on earth delayed. I will delay deaths and note down the karma of people till you come back to take their lives."

14.

Surya-Sabha

"What is this?" Indrani who was trying to console a crying Tapti, asked as Yami explained the situation. These three occupied a corner in Surya's court with Varuna standing there, trying to assess everything.

The other devas who had arrived at Suryaloka in a hurry were quietly observing two very awkward scenarios. First was Shani being engaged with Surya in what seemed like a heated argument and though both looked enraged, the younger lad was the on verge of a breakdown.

The second awkward scenario was two exactly identical goddesses standing in the middle of the hall with their heads lowered down. Devi Sanjana had married Surya ages ago, but no one ever heard about her being a twin, so obviously this is a fantastical absurd situation.

"I would take the lead for now, please pay attention to me." A hesitant voice came from the dais. Yamuna had taken a stand, she had always been headstrong and energetic, so others fell completely silent upon seeing her. Varuna gave her a nod of encouragement.

Returning back to Tapti and Indrani, he whispered to them- "If anything extreme happens, both you sisters will immediately leave with me to safety."

The queen rubbed the shoulders of a now calm girl, "Look, Varuna dev love you children and so do I, in case things go out of hand, my husband would intervene with his authority." she spoke kindly.

Yamuna continued with her speech, ignoring the chatter from the corner- "One of the two women whom you all see standing here is Devi Sanjana, the legit wife of my father Surya Deva. The other identical woman is Devi Chhaaya, the clone who my mother created from her shadow."

"Devi Sanjana joined our father in matrimony, gave birth to Yami and Yama. But she couldn't bear the heat of Surya deva and so she left in secret to find a cure for this. Meanwhile, she had left Chhaaya in her place to fulfil her duties and hide her absence." Shani said as he joined Yami at front.

"And the one I considered my love, my partner, the mother of all my children, the one I considered my wife Sanjana, was just her reflection. Chhaaya lived with me all this time, she gave birth to Shani and Tapti, all this time I was being fooled." Surya was exhausted, sinking deeper into his throne.

Tapti who has gained her composure saw this as her chance to finally speak up. "Surya Patni, Devi Sanjana abandoned her husband and children in the care of her shadow. All this time the one who served Suryadeva dutifully and was a mother to Yama and Yami was Chhaaya, while also she bore me and my twin Shani as our biological mother. Devi Sanjana has finally returned today, demanding her place back and for Chhaaya to merge with her. Chhaaya, refuses all that and is asking to stay. Who is the right one here?" Tapti was expectant of others, she wanted a solution to the chaos, glancing at Devendra whose primary duty was to solve all conflicts among devas.

Devaraja Indra catching the cue walked to centre, "Partially I understand the situation of your family Tapti but let us hear out both the women first. Starting with Devi Sanjana."

"My fault for creating Chhaaya. I made her for one purpose alone, to take care of my husband and children while I am gone to do penance. I craved the love of my husband but his touch left burns, I couldn't bear the heat of living here. I didn't expect my own shadow to betray me." Sanjana was angry.

"I served Surya Deva with love and devotion, with him I bore my own children Tapti and Shani but that never made me partial towards Yama and Yami. My motherhood is taintless, I was maternal to them all equally, I consider Surya Deva my husband. After all these years, how can I leave this family? Why must I go back?" Chhaaya was desperate, crying.

Devendra was taken aback by the raw emotions of both the sides, he looked towards Indrani with almost pleading eyes. She took the lead, "Ever since I have been married to Devendra, I have seen Devi Sanjana as my friend and now I see it was Chhaaya all along. I have seen the children of Suryaloka grow from their toddlerhood to adolescence and I testify that Chhaaya was a loving mother to them all. I am also a witness to the married life of Surya and Chhaaya and it was truly pure. It is unfair to not let her continue the way she has lived."

Shani and Chhaaya were equally relieved now that Devarani had took a stance in their favour. Devaraja and Surya seemed to be dismissive.

"I only created Chhaaya for a specific purpose and fixed period of time, she took care of my children, and I will raise hers. But I will not share my husband. Chhaaya should merge back with me." Sanjana was adamant.

Devendra took her side- "Devi Sanjana is the legally wedded wife of Surya deva, we all witnessed their wedding. Devi Chhaaya, any relation you had with him should be considered illicit and Sanjana is your creator, owner, master, and you shall not deny her, please go back to where you have come from."

Indrani was first to disagree with her husband- "No, Devi Sanjana abandoned her family first and now she expects Chhaaya to do the same. Is love, respect and service not enough proof of matrimony? Did the shadow of Sanjana not marry Suryadeva along with her?"

Devendra glared at his wife, "None of that matters. Chhaaya was created for a purpose and now when her work is done, let her leave. Devi Sanjana shall be restored to her rightful place."

Indrani lowered her eyes, she knew well that disagreements with Indra have become futile. He has grown in glory, valour, and pride so the opinions of others were meaningless to him now. But smartly enough she shifted the court dynamic, "My lord, your words remain undeniable, but this matter affects Suryadeva the most. Shouldn't the final decision be his?"

Indra pleased by his wife's speech, allowed Surya to take the lead back.

"Both Sanjana and Chhaaya gravely betrayed me. Sanjana is the one married but no moment with Chhaaya is regretted by me. And both of them lied. Gave me four children and all this time I didn't know the truth. As Indra said, none of that matters, so I deny you both the title of my wife. I loved both but, in this moment, I know neither."

15.

Chhaaya-Martand Shani

Chhaaya devi deeply aghast by the words of Surya who had just now disowned both Sanjana and her shadow, stood there dumbfounded.

Chhaaya walked closer to Sanjana, babbling wildly "All I ever did was serve. To your husband, a wife. To your children, a mother and how now I realise that I am not a person of my own. For my final act of service to you now devi, take me with you."

It took not a moment for Chhaaya to become the shadow of Sanjana again. She was made of flesh till now but became an inky black picture and nothing more. Varuna submerged Yami and Tapti within him taking both his nieces to the safety of water, flow that was the nature of ocean god and river goddesses. He knew what would follow.

Shani's eyes blackened with blind rage he could no longer see or hear anything. Surya ran quickly to Sanjana, collapsing on the floor near her. Why? He asked both the woman and her shadow.

Sanjana walked away ruthlessly, "She wasn't your wife, I am." Opening her arms to Shani in a welcoming gesture, she said "You came from Chhaaya thus you came from me. You are the only child of mine who stands in front of me, please come to me. I am your Maa, don't look like that. Your father has rejected me as his wife, but I cannot bear being away from my children. Please my child, please for once." It was only in this moment she would have cried but didn't.

Shani broke down in the moment completely, "You are not maa, my mother was Chhaaya. She was the rightful wife of my father. Bring her back, she deserves to be here. NOT YOU DEVI SANJANA!"

"Your mother was no one's wife. She was no one at all. She was characterless woman who stole my husband, slept with him in my place. I accepted you as my stepson but now I doubt. Are you even a son of Surya? What if that low charactered wench slept with some other man to have you? How can you be the seed of Surya and be this savage?" Sanjana laughed hysterically, the entire sabha gasped.

Indrani felt a pang of rage but was stopped by Indra before she could react. Varuna had left already, and the other devas knew better than to interfere now.

Shani reacted before anyone else could see what has happened. With his left leg, he kicked the womb of Sanjana who screamed with pain and went down on her knees. "Thank Mahadev for not making me take birth from that wretched womb of yours." He was furious, Surya didn't even flinch.

Shani turned to his father, "My mother gave birth to me with your seed and yet you didn't speak as she left? Why did you not defend the honour of Chhaaya devi? Surya deva, you failed me." The boy's eyes were fuming with blackness like that of charcoal.

Surya was darkening, he couldn't breathe anymore. The sun was eclipsed as Shani kept drawing all the powers from his father's body.

"Look now Devi Sanjana, you couldn't bear this very heat and abandoned your husband. I stand here taking all his tapa and teja within my eyes alone, is that not a proof that I am his seed? Surya deva is indeed my father but today I am ashamed of admitting so." Shani kept drawing all that he could from Surya who sat there with his eyes closed, he looked at peace. For a moment, he was cold even if he couldn't breathe.

Sanjana bewildered, still crouched, and held her womb in pain. "To show respect for your mother, you insulted motherhood itself. You kicked me in the womb, and I curse may that leg of yours be forever broken." She left the sabha immediately.

Shani who had stopped tormenting his father by now screamed in pain, exasperated, he went back to a foetal position. Curling his body, holding his knee to the chest, he cried slowly. The leg was breaking but the boy was broken completely.

While the other devas were quick to reach out for the father and the son, they both were profoundly lost in the hurt of betrayal.

Surya embraced Shani, trying to rub his hands. I am sorry, he kept muttering to his crying son. "Shani, the curse cannot be reversed or taken back but I can heal your leg, it won't break off completely, but you shall walk with a limp forever. And son, I bless you today though you are bound to be slow in gait, may you forever reach your destination on time."

The pain eased but the boy sobbed, he clanged on to his father, "Baba, maa?" he asked. "You have always provided me with whatever I asked for, please bring mother back." He cried more. "Please bring back maa, the way you healed my leg, heal my heart too please!"

Surya gestured others to leave as he sat there rocking his child who cried uncontrollably, "Sorry my son, I am sorry for everything. I cannot bring back your maa, forgive me."

Before he could soothe the boy any longer, Shani got up and went straight to the window. Crying he called for his only friend, a giant crow. Shani sat on his mount, he ordered the crow to fly faster.

Surya's response was to call for his chariot. "Aruna Deva, you must follow Shani fast! Stop him before he goes berserk." He ordered the charioteer.

Shani had reached Kailasha once again, he kept invoking the one whom he considered the supreme godhead, but Mahadeva who refused to bring Chhaaya back was then attacked by her son.

All knowing Shiva had hit Shani with his trident causing him to faint on spot, he looked almost lifeless. Surya who had witnessed all of it begged Shiva, "Please spare the life of my son. Had I ever been of service to the world, have mercy on me Mahadeva. Please let him live."

Shiva who expected all these events, declared- "Shani was born to you and Chhaaya as the fruit of my blessing. Your child will live but the condition is I will become his guru, Suryadeva, leave him here and go back to your duties. I will return your son when the time comes."

16.

Dharmaraja Yama

The Chaturbhuj Bhagwan Narayan stood in front of me. I have seen him in person before then why am I crying at his sight? Is this what devotion does to heart? I felt content, looking at his lotus, chakra and gada. I know him, he looks so much like my father. I am satisfied.

"Stop crying child. I am pleased by you, ask for anything and I shall grant it today." He speaks with ease, but I genuinely want nothing from him.

"You! I will serve you for an eternity that's all I ask for." My tongue rolls on her own, the words I didn't think of, are expressing my heart's desire.

He chuckled, I feel childish but satisfied, "Very well but how? I can give you the throne of Indra, would you want to replace him? Or you can easily become more powerful than any other deva." Narayan really is offering everything but no.

"I don't care about power. I am the god of death itself and Narayan, you know best that death sees nothing. Death has no regards for power, pleasures, looks, health, status. Death has no mercy or brutality, it is the only truth for those who live. Devaloka, it is best if I have less involvement there, Pitruloka waits for me to rule it." My answer was earnest, he smiled.

He blessed- "Then I grant you the title of Dharmaraja, I preserve the universe and Indra rules it. I establish the dharma and you shall rule it from now on. Be the pinnacle of the righteousness and rightfulness."

"I am grateful beyond words but allow me to return home now. My family must be waiting for me in Suryaloka, and I will- oh" what halted me completely was my hands touching the horns over the head.

After these many years, I almost forgot what brought me here- the ugliness. This face, I am ashamed of showing it to my pita. Dhumorna, she never liked me back when I was handsome, will she even glance at me now that I am a monster?

Narayan who had read my mind, spoke again "Yama, these horns of yours, place them on the first animal you see, and that species will take the burden from you forever. Mahadeva was lenient in his curse, go look at yourself, you have outgrown that appearance and grown into a fine man."

After leaving through the gates of Vaikuntha, I kneeled on the shore of Ksheer Sagara. My reflection in the water was unrecognisable. The fat became muscle mass, this body is identical to Surya deva and the facial hair look groomed, the spots and scars on my skin have vanished.

As I got up, I saw a creature bathing in the water. Four legged, tailed, a land animal. When it saw me getting closer, it bowed down. Lowering his head and eyes as a gesture of respect, I liked it.

"What animal are you?" I asked. "A buffalo, water buffalo, my lord. I was waiting for you." It replied, he sounds like a male.

"Why?" I inquired taken by surprise. "Because I have heard about you the lord of death and the dead. I swore to serve you as I oversaw you immersed in penance." He walked closer, I petted his head. How sweet, I love him already.

Taking my horns that came out in hands, I placed them on the buffalo, it suits him. "Though your kind will bear the burden of my horns, this curse of mine shall bless you all. This horns will help you defend your tribe even if a lion comes attacking."

The happy animal licked my hands, I used to be disgusted back when young but now this feels like an act of pure affection. "You wanted to serve me? become my companion then. I grant you the status of becoming my symbol, my dhwaja, my vahana."

"Lord, please allow me to carry you back to Suryaloka." He said.

17.

Nyay-adheesh Shani

"So now I have become Nyayadheesh, the lord of justice." This is me trying to confirm my own designation that I just now received.

Mahadeva nodded slightly in a yes, his eyes remained close in meditation. Such was my guru and aradhya who rarely spoke and remained deep in meditation. "And my purpose is to count the deeds of all, the karma of everyone, be it devas, asuras, manushya or whatever?" I asked, he nodded again.

"And I will grant the consequences of one's actions. To punish the wrong deeds and reward the right ones is my job now?" this was my third question, Shiva opened his eyes.

"Yes, and now you officially get to do half of Yama's work. You shall do for the living, what he does for the dead." Mahadeva has a hard to decipher tone, he is too innocent to be sarcastic or maybe not.

"What does that mean? I am the lord of karma and justice." Looking at Shiva's face that remains neutral, I know he is laughing on the inside.

"Yes, and your brother whom I made the lord of death has also become the lord of dharma just now by Narayan's grace. Leave now, your family is waiting." He commanded.

"Gurudeva, I don't have a family or home to return to. Mother, brother, sisters they left me behind and then I left my father." My tears dried long ago, though there is no more crying, but the sadness lingers in the mind.

He laughed, Shiva laughed outright. "Chhaaya, Sanjana both my devotees. Your mothers are by the side of your father. Do you not want to meet them? Yama, Yami, Tapti, Revanta and Ashwini Kumaras, all your siblings would be waiting for you." He said before shutting his eyes again.

"I am leaving for Suryaloka immediately then." Whistling summoned my friend of solitude, my loving crow. The giant Himalayan black bird that once brought me here will now take me back home.

While boarding the bird that decided to be my vahana, I looked back at Mahadeva "Who is Revanta and who are those whatever kumaras you speak of?" This was the final question I asked and knew better than to expect the answer, Shiva chose silence over all languages. I will now have to solve this new mystery in Suryaloka.

18.

Surya

Noisy, Suryaloka is exceptionally noisy today. "Baba, how could you do this to us? It is so unfair." Shani was back at calling out all that he deemed unfair, when he first came back, I was surprised looking at his face and demeanour but not much has changed. Now that he is the justice giving deva, him calling something unfair has become extreme.

"My brother is right, we left only for a few years, and you gave our rooms to the other twins? Those Ashwini Kumaras or whatever their names are shouldn't be taking over our place." Yama has unionised with Shani again, I suppose they are reasonably shocked.

"Your place? This is our loka, our family. Why don't you two go back where you came from?" Revanta who is the angry one interjected, he is the youngest child I have as of now.

I facepalmed, lounging back on the chair. Dasra brought me a bowl of syrup. He and his twin have been experimenting with medicinal science and always I am their subject.

"Are you feeding poison to my father?" Shani was staring at us with disdain. "No, it is called medicine. You would have known about had you not skipped your classes with Devaguru Brihaspati." Dasra is equally rude in his replies.

"Yeah, his guru is Shiva who made Brihaspati the guru of devas in the first place. Why are you so proud of your little potions." Yama is not happy either.

"Potions? I, Nasatya, and my twin Dasra were blessed by Brahma deva to become the physicians of devas." Nasatya is gentle in voice but has a temper.

"We Ashwini Kumaras, were born with the healing powers of the Sun. We were taught by Rishi Dhadhici the greatest devotee of Shiva." Dasra enjoys casually boasting his achievements, he is just like Yama.

"Baba, which pair of brothers is less annoying? Shani and Yama OR Dasra and Nasatya?" Trying to put all others down at once, only Revanta dares say such things. He and Shani are alike in speech.

"The only pair I like are my daughters. Can you boys not become calm, gentle, and sweet like your sisters? Tapti is so sophisticated, Yami is everyone's favourite." My words have hit the right spot, there is collective groan of disappointment.

Fatherhood is an integral part of my being and I will never regret this.

THE BOOK OF MAHABHOOTS

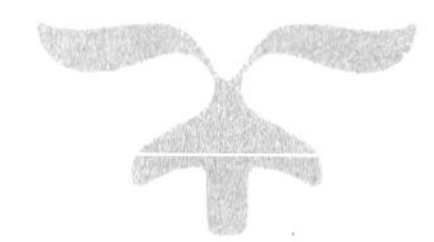

VAGRANT

19.

Surendra

There exists not a single mind capable of comprehending how difficult it is to be the king of gods, the ruler of all worlds alone. It would be difficult enough to spiral anyone who desires my throne into a hurricane of tragedies. But not for me, I was born to do this, I am made to be the king, anointed as the Devaraja, I alone am capable of wearing this crown.

However, when I witnessed what happened to Yama, the fact that even gods like us are doomed to perish has sunk much deeper into me. I wouldn't die, I never lose but the other devas, if even one of them goes out the cosmos will be thrown out of balance and that is what I cannot afford.

I wish the devas could work a day without one of them causing trouble or receiving a curse but alas! I am so done with them all.

Yama became the god of the death itself; he remains the only one who will never experience death again but what about the day his noose starts sucking out the life from other devas?

Shani's eyes are still a problem, he was born with that dreadful gaze, but the power only grows out of control. Just like the powers of Surya, he is burning so much, he might end up exploding or at least start burning almost everything to the ashes. He is my brother; without him the world dies but if he doesn't find a cure to his teja then the world dies as well. Which end of the universe would be less painful? One without the sun or one because of the sun. Vayu says he has trouble controlling all the gasses now that people breathe more but pollute the air even more. Manushya-jati, the humans we created with love, it has been a few years of their existence and I can tell they are more chaotic than Asuras ever will be.

Those humans have already forgotten their creators, have they? They worship me for rain but have been cutting all the forests that my rain grows. They worship Varuna on the seashores and riverbanks but the waters they pollute is turning Varuna sick. Varuna, my brother used to be so angry when even one of devas would do harm to any fish as an accident, now he is worshipped everyday by humans who kill the marine life without remorse.

Surya is who they wait for every day, they worship him the most. All over that green blue planet, they worship Surya like anything, yet these humans complain about the heat. And they cry about how dark their nights are.

What is the most frightening aspect is that these humans are still those with divine memories. They are living in the Kruta-yuga, the satyuga. They know Brahma as their creator, they hold the power to someone any of us devas with their prayers. Then why are they like this? And I know this cycle is eternal but after this Kruta-yuga will appear Treta, Dwapar then at the end Kali-yuga and oh my! The age of Kali is always the most dreaded by us.

Even though Sri Hari will keep restoring the balance time and time again when things go out of hand and ultimately Mahadeva will suck all the creation within him during the Mahapralaya. Aren't we devas the most overworked from Satyuga to Kali age?

When has Agni or Varuna ever abandoned humanity? When have I ever not served the gods and the humans? Then why am I the arrogant one? Why do they villainise me the most when I own the very universe, they all exist in? Yes, I am filled with pride to the brim but who else other than me deserves to be this proud?

I am Indra, Devraja Indra. I am worthy of the praises the praises that are sung in my honour. Glory to me, forever and ever.

20.

Agniphera

It has been years now since Indra and his loka, received their beloved queen. Indra and Indrani ruled the heaven with the best of their capabilities but what made a few envious was how loving their couple had become.

Indrani known for her beauty, charm, charisma, and authority over the arrogant king Indra had drawn enough attention to herself that not only were people envious of her but in fact Indra became popular as the goddess of pride and envy. This reputation went well with her danavi origins. To Indra though, Indrani was a pious woman whom he ultimately surrendered too, and this love was what made many others desire something similar.

Agni dev had grown lonely and tired. When in Indraloka, he would watch Indra and Indrani being close to each other and the fire god was longing for something similar. Surya for instance had a big and loving family, a wife and children which made his life complete. Even Varuna was always busy taking care of the marine life, the fishes, and other aquatic beings which he considered no less than children. Vayu was friends with almost every bird that existed.

Mostly alone, Agni longed for companionship. The saptrishis, the seven sages who were most revered for their austerities and penance came together to perform some important Yajnas. This Yajna would ultimately favour the gods and knowing this Agni was tasked by Indra to stay with the rishis in their ashram.

Agni who while representing the Pasupathi aspect of Shiva was now present in the Saptarshi Ashram in the form of Yajna Agni. There existed nothing in this entire universe, which is purer than sacrificial fire, thus when Agni became Yajna-Agni he attained the most pious form possible for him.

Among the seven sages, Maharishi Vishwamitra alone was the unmarried one. Maharishi Agastya was married to Lopamudra who was eldest among the wives of the saptrishis. Then there was Maharishi Atri whose wife was Mahasati Anusuya. Likewise, Maharishi Bhardwaj was tied to devi Susheela.

Maharishi Gautam's wife was Ahalya and Maharishi Jamdagni was married to devi Renuka, but it was the wife of Maharishi Vasistha, Arundhati the most beautiful and divine among the six wives of the six rishis.

Married men are never to perform a yajna or any other act that which was sacred in the absence of their wives. Hence, the six out of the seven celestial sages would sit around the Yajna-Agni alongside their wives. Witnessing the beauty of those holy women infatuated Agnidev who being aware of the sinful nature of his lust has run away from the Ashram.

The sages being wiser than even the devas knew about the events of the future; they weren't keen on finding where Agni had ran off to.

The fire god, had by befriended an interesting goat like creature, known as the Ram. Rams are powerful, round horned, and stubborn but most importantly they revered Agni as their patron deity and protector.

Agni who now rode his favourite ram, was riding fast towards a jungle. There was nothing but lust in his mind, something he wanted to clear. How could the god of sacred rites be infatuated by the holy wives of saints and sages? Oh, what shame!

Deep inside the woods, he sat in meditation unaware of the two sharp eyes that were staring at him. It was a woman, sharp and cunning. She had the eyes of a fawn and the mind of a fox and most dangerously had her eyes fixed on the fire god.

Svaha, the daughter of Daksha Prajapati and his queen Prasuti was born with a rebellious heart. Daksh and Agni had their differences due to their faith towards Shiva and Svaha was aware of this.

This woman was as infatuated by Agni as he was by the wives of those rishis but most importantly what Svaha wanted was to play with fire. Proud of her wits and arts of disguise, Svaha wished to seek the approval of Agni, whom she considered to be the supreme most god.

Agni would try going deeper into his meditation, thinking of ways to purify himself until he saw Lopamudra walking towards him. The wife of Rishi Agastya. Surprised to see Lopamudra trying to seduce him, Agni lost control over his senses. Not being able to think about the rights and the wrongs, Agni made love with Lopamudra who went back and vanished in the woods.

The cycle repeated next day, this time with Atri's wife Anusuya. Another day it was Susheela, then Ahalya and Renuka and so five days had passed. On the sixth day, all Agni did was wait for Arundhati to satisfy what should have remained of his lust. Unfortunately, the fire's hunger grows more as you feed it.

Arundhati appeared, a woman only second to Indrani in her beauty. Agni whose desire for intimacy had only increased in the past five days was too quick to catch her.

He made love to the woman, he felt there was no reason for him to stop. Even though Svaha's disguise fell off because she too was unable to embody the divinity of Arundhati, Agni continued what he did with Svaha.

Hours and days passed, and his ultimate thirst of Kama was thus quenched, looking at Svaha, the

woman who was shivering in his arms; he asked-
"And so who are you?"

Svaha who was too overtaken by Agni was only now realising that she stood as herself and not as someone else, the reality of her disguise falling off long before, only now caught up to him.

"Daughter of Daksha Prajapati and Queen Prasuti, I came here to tempt you O devagni." Her voice was confident but heart too shy to face Agni directly. "Do you not have a name?" the fire god asked staring at the woman. "I do and you may call me Svaha." She said finally making an eye contact. The name Svaha charged something primal inside Agni, he knew in a minute that Svaha was his shakti, the way Poulomi was Indra's.

"Svaha." He chanted the name a few times, the ring of it seeped deeper in his body. "Next time when you come to me, come as yourself Devi Svaha, I know now that no woman other than yourself is capable to satisfy my lust." He said, Svaha turned her face away in embarrassment, she realised now what her rebellion had made her do.

"Oh, Svaha, why don't you become for me what Arundhati is to Vashishta." He asked trying to hold her closer. Svaha nodded a few times in confusion, "come with me" she told Agni before taking him to the riverbank of Ganga.

On the bank of Ganga, there was kept a pot of gold, a vase that was glowing with divine beauty. "What is it?" Agni asked raising his eyebrows, hush Svaha gestured as she placed her hands over the pot transferring some energy into it.

"You made love to six times in total, I brought whatever amsa, teja, seed and divinity left of you inside my body here to keep it collected in the pot." Agni kneeled touching the pot that kept glowing, he could tell it wasn't just his amsa alone, but a part of Svaha's courage and rebellion was visible through it. "Today was the sixth and you did so for the last five times?" he confirmed, Svaha nodded.

Ganga who till now flowed with silence manifested as a woman through her waters. Agni and Svaha greeted her with respect.

"Devi Svaha, both daughters of Daksha, you and your sister Sati were aspects of Shakti. Though Sati gave up her body in Agni itself, remember now she has come back as Parvati, my sister born to Himavan and Maina." Ganga reintroduced the dynamics of the three present there, making them aware of what really was happening.

"All six of these mingled energies that come from the lustful and loving union of Svaha, aspect of Shakti and Agni, aspect of Shiva, let these six energies be given to me for I will raise them as a foster mother. Let Parvati be the mother to what both of you have created." Ganga spread her arms in front of Svaha who held the vase even tighter. Ganga laughed at the ignorance of the devi.

"Oh Svaha! My sister Parvati was your sister Sati in her previous life, she was cursed by Rati the wife of Kama deva to never bear a child in her womb. This pot has aspects of Shiva and Shakti's energy, this union which satisfied the Kama within you two, let it satisfy the motherhood of Parvati." Saying this Ganga pointed at the six full bloom lotuses that floated upon her waters.

Agni taking the six balls of energies which looked something similar to foetuses, placed each of them upon the lotuses. Surrendering the child to Shiva, he took Svaha with him to the Saptarshi Ashram. The rishis were waiting for them both.

Svaha and Agni were married in the presence of the seven divine sages and the six holy wives blessed the couple that without Svaha, Agni would become incapable of burning anything and the name of Svaha must be invoked to make any offerings to the fire.

The six balls of energies slowly became six identical boys who combined together into one, forming the six headed god, nursed on the constellation of Krittika known as Pleidas by Matrikas and the six wives of rishis.

This six headed boy was Skanda, the god of war Kartikey who became victorious by slaying the evil Tarkasura. Whether the world calls him to be son of Mahadeva and Parvati or the son of Agni and Svaha, Skanda in his raw essence is who emerged out of the union of Shiva and Shakti, symbolising the satiated Kama, he was the god of masculinity, purusha tattva itself. Hailed eternally as the son of Krittikas, know him as Kartikey. Raised by the matrikas, he is eternal victor of every war.

21.

Sham No Varunah

Rishi Atri, a highly revered sage, was born directly from the mind of Brahma, the creator, into this world. His wife, Mahasati Anusuya Ji, was an even more respected figure among all. She was the epitome of chastity, a pious woman whose loyalty had never wavered, not even in her imagination, from her husband. Yet, she harboured a deep wound – the pain of being childless.

Despite Atri and Anusuya's intense longing to have and raise a child of their own, their wishes remained unfulfilled. That was until Durvasa, the most intimidating sage of all time, feared even by the gods, emerged from Shiva's rage. As a form of Shiva, Rishi Durvasa had fulfilled Anusuya's motherly instincts, but as he grew, he gradually distanced himself, pursuing his own path. Now, suffering from the pain of an empty nest, a devastated Anusuya turned to her husband: "This loneliness curses me. I yearn for another child, and you are the only one who can provide it." Her voice was stern and rough.

"Beloved, you and I both know it's impossible," Atri replied, acknowledging his wife's vulnerability. "What do you want me to do?" He asked. "You are the son of Brahma, the creator of the universe itself," Anusuya pleaded. "He is the writer of destiny. Can you not take my prayers to him? Can you not ask your father to bless me with another child?" Atri obliged, moved by his wife's words.

Brahmaloka, the residency of the creator, the womb from which all existence is manifested; that is where Brahma resides with his consort, Devi Saraswati. Pearly white clouds, where Brahmadev was enthroned on a blooming lotus, looked down at Atri, who had just entered the place and stood before him. "I know already why you are here," said the creator. "And so, would you fulfil the only desire of our tiring hearts? My wife and I want nothing more than to have a child of our own again." Rishi Atri seemed intent.

"Your destiny will cross paths with two more children in the future; both will grow up to call you, their father. You have Durvasa in the image of Shiva; you will be blessed again with a son in the image of Vishnu in the future, but now is the right time for you to have a son in my image. Are you ready to receive him?" This was a declaration by Brahma but posed as a question. Atri, having no reason to object, had agreed, and thus the craftsmanship of the creator was used again.

Brahma, the old man with four heads and four faces looking in the four opposite directions, embodied the imaginative aspect of God. Now, from his hands, shining white light with little hues of blue kept emerging as he crafted a baby boy. The eyes of

Brahma were filled with tears. The joy this unfinished and unborn child brought to Brahma was incomparable, putting together his own essence in the flesh of an infant must have been a different kind of pleasure. He cried so much that the child remained unfinished.

"I apologize; I cannot complete him. This is overwhelming even for me," said Brahma, looking at Atri, tears staining his cheeks and dampening his white beard. "You cannot do this to my father. I need this boy; I wish to raise my son. How will I ever return empty-handed back to my wife? Anusuya would feel crushed. I will not return till I have my child." These determined words of Atri made the creator begin again.

This time, in the hands of Brahma, slept a newborn, freshly crafted, he who didn't come out of a womb. The baby was beautiful, more radiant than anything else in the world, and cold to touch. Even the eyes of those who had made him were shut close, and there was light emitting continuously from his flesh. He was bright, almost like the Sun, but he had this beauty and innocence that was overwhelming to touch.

"He is born, O Atri, but now, even if you wish, you cannot take him home. Look at him, alive and breathing, but he seems way too divine. He has this radiance, which I deem the cosmos is unready to receive. This boy of immense power and glow must be kept a secret from the world. I know the glory that lies in his destiny, and though he is your son, you cannot raise him like one, at least till he is much older."

"What do you mean, father?" asked Atri, a bit shocked, as he continued, "Will he not be nourished by his mother's milk? Will he not learn how to walk by holding my finger? Why did you give me hope and this child a life when your plan was so cruel?"

Brahma said, "He has a greater purpose; being your son is just his way, or perhaps my way, of fulfilling your desire. Trust my word; take this baby of yours to Ksheer Sagara; let Vishnu do what he always does – a leela."

The sole provider of light and life, Sun has already set. Surya deva had retreated to his realm to get his rest. Now in the pitch-black night, all alone stood Atri with a swaddled infant in his arms on the shore. Ksheer Sagara the richest ocean is the divine realm of Varuna Deva, the god of waters and all that lives within it.

Each wave is a masterpiece, and, on the surface, there lies Vaikuntha, the home to Vishnu. In his four arms, the preserver, provider, and protector of the universe and all its creations- Vishnu, held a mace, a lotus, a conch, and a disk. Varuna who thought of it as a duty to serve Vishnu, was the one who kept Vaikuntha afloat on the Sagara.

"I see you are here, Rishi Atri." Varuna greeted the sage with a namaste gesture. "Our great lord Vishnu has already instructed me about the matter. Hand your son over to me and be assured that I will keep him nourished the same way you and your wife would have." Said Varuna.

"This child, my son. I was told to bring him here as I am not allowed to keep him." Atri was using all his strength in holding back his tears, his shoulders softened as he handed over the baby to the water god. "Why?" He muttered.

"I cannot tell you because I too am ignorant about the future. But I have been commanded by Lord Vishnu, and you, Rishivar I deeply respect. I will take this child with me, raise him in my realm. My waves will be his world till he has to return."

Saying this the god of oceans turned around. His feet left no footprints on the shore, only wetness. His legs became one with water and the baby boy disappeared in the depths. Silently praying to Vishnu, Atri left for his home.

Years passed and the baby grew into a youthful boy. Always floating deep inside the ocean serenely. He never had to swim; he couldn't drown. He had no concept of anything, just stories told by Varuna to pass his time. "What is the world above your water like?" He had asked once to which the ocean replied- "Dark, very dark. It used to be dark here too but since you came, I have been glowing."

The little one giggled, "You lie Varuna, I have seen the golden light that reaches me during the day. It's so warm unlike you. I wish I could touch it."

Varuna chuckled- "That golden light is sunshine, Surya is the bestower of it."

The boy curious inquired again- "But who is Surya? And why won't you let me go above and beyond to meet him?" Varuna, the entire ocean itself seemed defeated. This water god could never cry, he could flood all the realms but when sad, his tears would dry. In a disappointed tone, he said - "NO. You are the son of Atri, Grandson of Brahma. You reside in and with me through the order of Vishnu and till he permits, you will neither see the light nor the world outside."

"I am imprisoned in your waters, but you are the only family I have. Atri is only a name that I know, you are my father- Varuna Deva the one who has always protected me. Anusuya to me is a story, but the milky waters of this ocean, this Ksheer Sagara is my mother. I don't want to leave you because of others." The boy was earnest in his words, his voice quivering.

"Chandra, you know well both you and I are the emotional type, then why torment my heart with your words. You are not leaving me today. As for the golden light, we might someday touch it together."

22.

Vayunah-Pranaha

I lowered my gaze as soon as Indrani entered Amravati. Ah this garden has become a remarkable beauty since her arrival, back when Indra lived alone, Indraloka was a dreadful and dry palace, golden but lifeless. How I wish Indrani could've change Indra the way she changed this place!

"You called and I came, how can I help you, Deva Vayu?" She sounds poised and humble at the same, unlike Devendra.

Sitting at a dignified distance, I greeted the queen and went off with my concern, "Devarani, do something about Devaraja. He is unserious in the sabhas and overworks us all tirelessly. Always treating us as we are beneath him, so we are but none of us Devas can sit here and take his attitude any longer." I heard her sigh.

"I was practicing Archery before your arrival. Archery even though I am an incredible swordswoman, do you know why?" She seems tired, maybe handling our courts haven't been easy for her lately, I nodded.

"I asked for my husband for a playful duel, and he ridiculed me instead. For your king, there is no greater warrior then him and a woman like me shouldn't even dream of sparring with him. He recounted the story of millions of asuras he killed, boasting his valour." Indrani is as frustrated as us all. Even Devaguru has been on edge.

"He killed millions of asuras? Let me tell you one incident, O queen of heaven. Once, Indra ordered me and Agni deva to slay all the demons. We both followed the orders of the king and kept crushing all of them, but some of those demons went inside the ocean, taking refuge in Varuna and asking for his protection." Narrating those times, what a pain!

The queen was intrigued, she cued me to continue and so I did, "We respected the dignity of Varuna who had no choice. We are gods, we protect all those who surrender no matter who they are, and Devendra knows this best." Yikes, my eyes are getting blurry, tears!

"What happened then?" Indrani inquired.

"Your beloved husband, our king cursed both I and Agni dev to be reborn and take incarnation in human body. He didn't even kill any demon, we did, and we were cursed as a reward for not our code." I choked on my words, imagine Indra becoming his former self.

"What was the result of this curse?" She asked again. And I answered- "By the grace of all father Brahma, I, Vayu Deva took the reincarnation as Rishi Vashisht and Agni Deva took birth as Rishi Agastya." My voice cracked, Indra is either the greatest king or the greatest headache, he has only ever lived in those extremes.

"Oh really? And the world benefitted from that curse, no? Rishi Agastya and Rishi Vashisht are great sages, blame me for the curse and not blame yourselves for incompetency." This haughty voice and tone belonged to Indra who had just arrived with a few other devas here. Clearly, he is expecting to be praised by all of us again and not interested in holding a real court or conference.

"Dear wife of mine, why are you here dealing with matters on your own, isn't that my work?" Devendra spoke, Devarani shuddered. Poulomi was a caged but gutsy girl BUT Indrani is a free yet timid woman. Even now she looks intimidated by him.

"Indrani, I summoned you in my room and you ignored my order? It is me the crowned king of gods who will deal with their concerns, you are my woman! Why are you here?" This poor woman has hung her head low, she is embarrassed being scold in front of me despite being the queen.

"STOP CRYING, GO BACK TO RANIVAAS AND REMEMBER THAT ALL YOU SHOULD EVER WORRY ABOUT IS SHRINGAAR. LEAVE." Devendra is practically screaming, I cannot intervene in their marital matters either but have some courage, woman. Some husbands act like they own their wives, and by some, I mean the Asuras. This is not the acharan of devas, we are more embarrassed than Devarani.

I can see the other devas are not holding their head high either, this is just our way of silent protest, but this Indra hasn't even noticed. The woman was escorted by the maids and so the only sane head figure was sent away. The crime of our capable leader? Being the obedient wife of this arrogant man.

"Vayu deva, have you no shame telling my wife stories of my past? Why would you avoid me, your king and speak to the queen instead?" He screamed and I snapped.

"You will not speak to me in that tone, DEVENDRA! Your story? It is our story. Your crown, your throne, your realm, your heaven, everything here is about you, and I am tired."

He looks more amazed than taken aback, inappropriate reactions. "What even are you without me?" he challenged.

My guru Brihaspati intervened, "Indra and Vayu, let us decide who amongst you is more important. Look at that mortal, down there on earth." Devaguru produced a divine vision of a human, male, young and healthy.

"I ask all you, devas to take back whatever sense you have given him and observe what happens." Guru ji ordered. Indra was the only one laughing, other devas are still sane.

"I will take his wealth and material, let us see what happens." Kubera said as one flick of his hand destroyed all abundance of that man. Few years passed on earth but in heaven, only a minute.

The man lived miserably but Kubera out of mercy gave back him the wealth tenfold. We saw the misery of poverty and respected Kubera Deva for both his importance and generosity.

"I, Surya am the bestower of vision, let me take away his eyesight." The Sun god rendered the man blinded for a few months; some seconds passed here in Amravati. Blind man was miserable, but Surya restored his eyes and healed his ailments too.

"Let me take away his manhood, I, Varuna deva, the god of water is also the controller of sperm and giver of progeny." The water god, imbalanced the hormones and rendered the man impotent for some years, here after a few seconds, Varuna gave back his masculinity and even blessed him with a son and a daughter.

"Agni is in the voice of all, I the mouth of gods shall make him mute." Agni deva was quick to take away the voice of this man, he survived but remained miserable. Agni not only returned his voice, he blessed the man with talents of singing and debate. This mortal, I don't know whether to feel good or bad for him because Indra was next.

"I am the lord of Indris and senses, let me take away all his sensations and strength." Devendra worked and for years, we saw that man not being able to feel anything, no pleasure or pain. He was basically a corpse that was alive.

Is this Devendra? Isn't he also way above the senses? Probably why we all found him hollow, for a moment I pitied Indra.

It was my turn, I declared I would take away the breathe, the prana of the man. After all, it is me, Vayu deva, the sole authority of air, wind, and gasses, one breathes me and through me.

The mortal had died in an instant, as expected, he didn't get up despite me returning his breath. He had crossed over. Others looked at me, Indra was hiding his embarrassment.

"You are not a merciful god, Vayu. You killed a poor human. You couldn't return his breathing despite ruling the air." This was enough.

"Devendra, mark my words, you will regret your pride one day." I left after saying so.

23.

Mrit Sanjeevani

Years, decades, centuries passed under the rule of Indra and Indrani who with the help of Agni and Svaha completed hundred rituals of sacrificial fire. Brihaspati the chief guru and minister of the devas overlooked the hundred yajnas done by Indra, making Brihaspati the primary purohit in the entire universe. Devendra in return earned the name 'Shatakrato' the doer of hundred deeds.

Kartikey who was assigned to become the army general of gods rarely ever attended any sabhas since most of his time was spent in battle fields dealing with ferocious asuras. The devas grew tired of wars that happened almost daily, and now even defeating their enemies were fruitless since the asuras learned the art of reviving the dead.

Today, Indrani sat on the throne with Indra, the exhausted devas were waiting for Brihaspati to arrive in the sabha.

Shani and Yama who had by now grown out of their toddlerhood and attained their own asanas and status as devas were whispering to each other. "So, what exactly is the rivalry between our Guru and Shukracharya?" Yama asked looking at his brother who paid little attention to the decorum.

Shani looked around for a bit and murmured the story in a muffled voice, "Oh do you not know? Rishi Angiras who is the father of Devaguru Brihaspati was the guru of both Brihaspati and Shukra. But Rishi Angiras had only ever paid more attention to his own son, ignoring the calibre of Shukra even though he was much better student and more efficient scholar."

Yama nodded for a moment, "So Shukracharya was the academic rival of Brihaspati, and their teacher Rishi Angiras was a partial one?" Shani replied with a yes and "Shukracharya, is a genius much better of a teacher than Brihaspati ever will be?" This subtle voiced conversation was overheard by someone.

"Oh, right and how do you know so much about Shukracharya, child? He left for penance years ago and only returned some time back." A voice asked.

Shani was haughty in his answer, "I used to be close to him when I was young and have been meeting him in secret to take private tuitions, but you don't tell my father whoever you- oh! I am sorry, wait I can explain."

The voice belonged to Suryadeva, he was looking at the young adul who seemed to be frightened and embarrassed. "Shukracharya is my worst enemy too, and I thought I was enough of a teacher for you." Surya sounded disappointed, Shani refusing to make an eye contact left the sabha early.

Devaguru Brihaspati had finally arrived in the court of Indra, who had become even more conceited than before. "I have figured out what the asuras are really doing." Guru said as he went on to take his asana. Indra was the only one who didn't greet him which didn't go unnoticed by the sabha. "What is it?" Indrani asked, even she had started to disdain Devendra's attitude by now.

"Devarani, your former acharya Shukra, had perform severe penance to please Shiva and received the Mrit-Sanjeevani Vidya in return." Brihaspati replied looking intently towards Devendra who seemed to be intoxicated, lost in the pleasures of touching his wife the way he shouldn't in the middle of a royal court.

Devendra was praised as a warrior, ruler and now Shatakrato all the time by the devas, gandharvas and apsaras. While all hailed him as a hero, his own minister and his wife Brihaspati and Indrani grew disdain towards his arrogance. They both saw where Devendra's pride was leading him to but for now Asura's were the greater threat.

Devaguru was answerable to Indrani, he replied to her question hoping that her sensibility would produce a solution.

"Mrit-Sanjeevani is a vidya, an art that can bring back the dead to life by reciting mantras and using invocations. It is extremely difficult art to master but since Shukra has received it directly from Shiva, he is the perfect vessel to practice and teach it further."

"So, there is no point of killing the asuras anymore since they can come back to life anytime they want. Shouldn't we also receive this vidya and use it on ourselves?" Out of all the devas present in the court, Yama was the most interested in the topics of life and death.

"That was my plan, I am sending my son Kacha to Shukra's ashram." Guru declared and after some time the sabha was adjourned.

24.

Kacha

Brihaspati, a man of austerity and reserved in nature, by far had only one son from young and beautiful wife, Tara. This son was named Kacha, an extremely capable young man of intellect and sobriety, one who could easily navigate social etiquette and deal with any unexpected situation but most importantly, Kacha to Brihaspati was a boy born to serve higher purpose even if it meant to sacrifice him.

Devaguru was too selfish to risk the lives of any deva, his duty as the guru came first but he was ready to send off his son to the dangerous territory because as a father, he was selfless and dutiful. Exactly opposite to Angiras for whom being good to his own son preceded being good to the students.

Kacha, the handsome youth had reached the ashrama of Shukracharya who was training some other asuras in there. There, contrary to expectations of Kacha, he was received with warmth by Shukra and his daughter, Devayani.

Shukra was surprised to see the son of his Guru-bhai present in front of him. Shukracharya didn't realise why exactly the grandson of Angiras, his own preceptor, stood in front of him to become a disciple. "Why me? Why not learn from Brihaspati who was more favourited by our guru Angiras?" That's what Shukracharya had asked Kacha on their first meeting.

"Because Acharya, there is one man whose knowledge and noble skills of teaching are respected by my father. No one other than Brihaspati can ever admire your knowledge and so by him I was sent here." Kacha's response tugged to the soft corner in the heart of Shukra.

Shukra as the Asura-acharya and Brihaspati as the Sura-guru were men who rivalled each other with mutual respect and hatred. Yet what they never lost completely was a brotherly attachment to each other perhaps that is why despite the countless battles between the gods and anti-gods, these two remained unscathed forever.

Shukra took care of Kacha as his son, initiating him with mantras and teaching him the art of celestial warfare, there was Shukra who wanted to prove his worth and wisdom to not only to Kacha, but to Brihaspati and perhaps it was Acharya's way of showing gratitude to Angiras.

Devyani, the amogh-sundari, the cosmic beauty, the youthful daughter of Venus itself, Venus that which is Shukra was infatuated deeply by the brilliance of Kacha. Both Devyani's interest and Shukra's interest had made all other Asuras wary and jealous of Kacha.

They uncovered the real intention of Kacha to learn and receive Sanjeevani Vidya and revive the devas with it. This deeply upset them, enough to make them bloodthirsty.

Once Kacha had went to the forest, where he was killed and assassinated by the asuras. Fortunately, Devyani who noticed his absence brought his body back to Shukra.

The girl cried to her father so he had no choice but to use the Sanjeevani vidya to bring the dead Kacha back to life where he would go back to his regular disciple journey.

Second time, Kacha was killed again with fire, but from the ashes he was brought back to life since Devyani had threatened to die on the same fire of pyre as well.

Ultimately, the frustrated Asuras had caught up to Kacha again, beat him dead to pulp and mixed his flesh and blood in a goblet of liquor. The chalice of this wine of death was presented to an already drunk Shukracharya who drank his own disciple in a sip. Devyani wailed.

Kacha requested to be brought back to life from within the belly of Daitya-Mantri Shukra. Acharya would have to die to bring Kacha back to substance, but love is where Shukra fails.

Shukracharya had no other option left but to teach Kacha the vidya of Mrit Sanjeevani. First the knowledge was used by the Acharya, so Kacha came out ripping apart the belly of his guru and then Kacha had revived his beloved preceptor using the vidya. All of this happened for Sanjeevani.

The son of Brihaspati whose main purpose was accomplished was first to ask the permission to leave the ashrama and go back to his father, Acharya had obliged.

Devyani who stood in his way asked to marry Kacha but he in return has said, "Oh, foolish girl, I came out of your father's body who gave me a new life three times. Your father who is like a brother to mine, had treated me like his own son. I see you as nothing more than my sister and to marry you would be immoral. Let me leave."

A furious daughter of Shukra, the short tempered Devyani who knew of the devas plans was quick to curse the boy, "Oh Kacha, you have broken my heart turning blind to my all because you came seeking this vidya for the devas. I curse you so this Mrit-Sanjeevani becomes useless for you, may you lose all capacity to revive the devas if they die."

Cursing her in return, Kacha the undercover agent of the gods has come back to heaven. He was successful in his mission but ultimately failed, a twist in fate that challenged the sacrifice of Brihaspati.

How much must the guru of devas, trusted the acharya of daityas, where he was ready to let his son die? Was Brihaspati always sure that Shukra would have brought his son to life? Or was he willing to let go of his own child for the sake and benefit of the gods? Either way the devas could have never asked for a better Guru, preceptor, or minister. Brihaspati embodied the brahmagyan.

Kacha returning without the knowledge of Sanjeevani extinguished whatever flame of hope the devas had, leaving them with no other solutions.

25.

Indrani

"You called me, my lord?" I greeted my husband as I entered the garden of Amravati. "Ah! My little flower, come and serve me." he reeks of *madira*.

"Lord, when I first came in here as your bride. You were humble despite being the king of devas and now I don't know you. Why have you started drinking Madira like an addict?" I was desperate, wanting him to hear the disappointment in my tone.

"Nonsense! Indra is the one who is above all Indris, don't you know the meaning of my name, beloved? Come here, I desire you." It is true that no amount of alcohol can make him drunk, Devendra is intoxicated with arrogance and confidence.

Sitting by his side feels strange now, my head on his chest. God, I miss the old him so much. "Your heartbeats used to be rhythmic to the song of love." Afraid, I am afraid I have offended him again.

"Right and what do they sound like now?" to my surprise, he isn't angry. But the way he caresses my cheek and holds me so tight, something is off.

"The sound of your vanity." I said hoping he would release me. My gut feeling says this is wrong and I shouldn't be close to him today, please sober up I pleaded to him in silence.

He is digging his fingers so deeply in my flesh, his aggression scares me sometimes. He used to be so gentle but now.

"Puloman's daughter is as annoying as her father once was. It is strange how you talking like my worst enemy, makes me desire you more." He brings my father knowing I hate it.

"Let my deceased father rest, he is gone now." I am riling him up just so he acts normal. My intuition is making me anxious.

"If you make love to me, I will make you the mother of my children." The reverse has happened, I am too anxious and now too angry to be here.

"Devendra do not touch me till you learn humility." I threw his hands off and stood up. He tried grabbing my wrist again, "Saying no to me, your lord? How dare you? You are so full of yourself because I admire you a bit too much. There are Apsaras like Urvashi who would entertain me any day, yet I don't go to them because I love you."

"Please let me go, you are hurting me. You love me for what? Beauty? Body? I plead you go to Apsaras or Gandharvinis, but don't come near me since you cannot respect me as your wife." I was about to yank his hand off till I realise that someone was coming.

Rishi Durvasa, a revered sage had entered Amravati. I spotted him from afar, knowing his quick temper I sat back with Indra to his left side.

"Ah, remember your place now?" This gesture just added fuel to the fire of his conceit. I looked at him, nodding and pleading with my eyes to shut up.

"I love you so much right now. The taste of madira lingering in my mouth, the fragrance of the flowers you care for, the beauty of Amravati, your soft body to touch. Indris, senses, I rule them and so all this pleasure belongs to me." He is babbling.

"My lord, please stop talking. This is not the right time" I said trying to close his mouth with my fingers. He misread this gesture, a grave mistake.

"You want me to stop talking already? How impatient. So, do I follow you to the Ranivaas or will you prefer my side of the palace? I prefer my chambers…" he finally noticed the sage who was nearing us. Indra looked annoyed when he realised.

"Welcome Rishi Durvasa, how may I serve you?" He greeted the sage but didn't even get up to touch his feet. Devendra kept rocking the swing we were sitting on, this is disrespectful. But till my husband, the king doesn't greet, I cannot do that either. According to the code, I must follow only my husband but what is he doing?

"Oh Devaraja Indra, I see you and Devarani Poulomi are happy today and so am I. The news of you performing hundred yajnas and becoming Shatakrato had reached my ashrama today." Rishi Durvasa, the speaker of these words is in a good mood today.

"I see, you are welcome to stay here as long as you want Rishivar but before I serve you, I must serve my wife. You shall go inside the palace and be my guest, I will come at your service when I done with her?"

Am I dreaming? Or has Devendra really said something so foolish? Asking the rishi to wait while being so immodest. What does he take me for?

"Very well Indra. I see how changed of a man you are now, and it is best if I just leave. Still to show you respect, here is a present." Durvasa Rishi has tolerated more than I would have.

He is presenting my husband with a garland of flowers. That gesture has honoured me as his wife. But Devendra is not actually wearing it, he keeps staring at the garland.

"Rishi Durvasa, you could have waited for your turn in my palace. I told you I wanted to be with my wife, didn't I? But instead, you halt me, the king of devas and for what? These dull flowers! Look around you, Amravati is the capital of swarga itself, look at the flowers in my garden." Indra had crossed his limits with these words. My husband, who I am ashamed to call my husband at the moment has thrown the garland far in the open ground. Even Airavat who too has become full of pride is crushing those lovely flowers with his feet.

The Rishi wanted to show respect and admiration. My husband and our vahana has ruined everything and now it has happened.

What devaloka fears the most has happened, Durvasa is angry. He is furious. He has dropped the water from his kamandal in his palm.

"Devaraja Indra, your arrogance has blinded you! You fail Brihaspati as a student and Poulomi as a husband and now you have failed the devas as their king. I curse you with Varuna as my witness, may all that you are proud of begone!"

Rishi's curse left me stunned, but my husband paid no heed to it. "The curse is futile, do not worry about it. Come with me now and that is an order." That night was one of the most restless ones.

The morning I rushed to the court before he could, the devas were staring at me, and Brihaspati looked concerned. The news had spread throughout Swarga and my husband is late to his own sabha, he has zero regards to all that is happening.

26.

Indrasabha III

Every devta present in the sabha that day was tense, Varuna looked angry in a murderous way. "Where is Devendra?" He demanded in a tone unheard before.

Devarani hung her head low and soon after Devendra followed, "Stop shouting, I am here." holding the wrist of his wife, he almost scolded her- "Why did you come before me? You are supposed to walk behind me, always."

Now that Indra was sitting on his throne, he gestured others to take their asanas, but all attendees kept standing. Protest, he understood that the gods are now defying him.

"Why? Because of Durvasa's curse?" Devendra leaned forward, he kept staring at everyone till his met those of Varuna who made him lower his gaze.

Vayu stepped forward, "Surya's teja is exceeding the limits of tolerance and he cannot attend sabhas anymore. Did you look for a cure?"

He continued, "The asuras have Mrit-sanjaveeni and Kacha risked everything to get it for us, though he couldn't but did you ever try to find a solution."

Vayu was visibly irritated, he took a few more steps forward, enough to make Indra go wide eyed and stare at him. He spoke again-

"Surya defends us during the day, but nothing shines during the night, and we are left vulnerable. Have you ever tried to find an alternative? Devaraja Indra the only way we devas gain our strength was through the yajnas and ahuti accepted by Agni. The enraged rishis refuse to continue doing that, you gravely insulted their sage hood. And Agni himself is cursed to eat impurities now."

Vayu is thunderous, enough to bring lightening of Indra back to senses. Varuna glanced at Indrani, "Your wife has proven to be a much efficient and responsible ruler than you, but you refuse to see her as an equal. You, Devendra don't see your own shakti as equal, how will you ever treat us right?"

Varuna moved to middle of Sabha and bowed in every direction, he knelt in front of Brihaspati before getting up and declared- "I am sorry to my brothers, to all devas present here. This is not your fault, it is our king even though he has no respect for that crown we all do. Devaguru, forgive me for I am bound by the curse of Durvasa. And Devarani, if you want to save your mangalsutra or yourself then go back to Danavaloka before I engulf the pride of Indra."

Devendra shot up from his throne, he couldn't react other than being horrified. In a moment, he saw his wife leaving his side, and Varuna engulfing all within himself, he drew back in his breath the majestic elephant Airavat and the crown of Indra. The gold, silver throne were sucked by Varuna. The fantastical jewellery that the gods were wearing disappeared, Varuna himself was left with plain clothing and nothing more.

"I am going back to Narayan, I cannot bear to be in devaloka for another moment."

Indra was flabbergasted, he looked at Brihaspati for answers who chose to remain quiet.

"Is this right according to dharma?" he asked looking at Yama who was left with only his noose now, the answer- "Are you above the curse of a sage? Are you above the plight of your own subjects? You are not above dharma, and you deserve this."

Shani added his words, "This is your karma and the fruits you must bear, I promise that no one can help you now till your karma is over."

At last, Indra looked at Agni. "I was cursed by Rishi Bhrigu to become a witness of everything both right and wrong. I was cursed that even the impure shall be dumped in my fires and I will consume it no matter what. Now I am no longer fit to participate in yajnas, so I am leaving in search of Brahma."

27.

Pavaka-Agni

Agni was present in the ashram of Bhrigu who lived with his wife Puloma. Bhrigu and Puloma lived as husband and wife but never officiated their wedding with rituals. When Puloma was only a young girl, a rakshasa had seen her and was infatuated with her beauty. Later this rakshasa had found out about the where she lived with Bhrigu.

Bhrigu had gone off somewhere, pregnant Puloma was sitting in the ashrama all alone. The Rakshasa came and met with Agni first, he asked the fire whether Puloma and Bhrigu were officially married? NO, Agni had answered because he didn't recognise a marriage not officiated with traditional rites where fire is the witness.

The rakshasa abducted that pregnant lady and ran away with her, due to the fear and anxiety, the woman gave birth to her child midway. The child later named Chyavana had fell on the floor but since he was born with the brilliance of hundred suns, seeing him made the rakshasa crumble to dust.

Puloma and Chyavana came back to the ashrama where Bhrigu was distorted upon seeing their condition. He cursed Agni, "You the devagni who witnessed this wrongdoing and did nothing, may you become the consumer of all things pure and impure.

And I curse to be the witness of all acts even those of adharma where you wouldn't be able to intervene."

The distraught Agni who was now guilty refused to participate in any yajnas. Leaving behind all he cared for, he went into deep meditation seeking Brahma.

The creator Brahma deva appeared in front of him. He granted the blessing to Agni, "Oh Agni, I bless fire to become the purest element in existence. From now, all that consume no matter what shall be purified and thus nothing will defile you ever."

Now back to Devaloka, Agni had come only to find nothing in Swarga looked the same. Without the yajnas and ahuti given by sages, the devas grew weak and weaker. They started losing to the asuras.

As informed by Ashwini Kumaras, health is a form of wealth which the devas lost due to the curse of Durvasa. The asuras resurrected themselves with Mrit Sanjeevani, the devas were reaching their limits. Vayu lost his strength, Agni lost his valour, Surya lost his brilliance and Varuna refused to show his face. Kubera lost all the wealth, and the devas became 'daridra.'

The lost and hopeless Devas approached Vaikuntha and the pleaded to Narayana.

28.

Varuna

Who knew the ocean itself could sink? But I in the form of a deva did seeing the others come near Ksheer Sagara.

In a moment, I was summoned inside the gates of Vaikunth where Narayan lay leisurely on Shesh. This Naga is so gigantic and fearsome, I wonder whether his body is even a comfortable place to sleep on, but God is under no obligation to make sense to any mind.

I frowned. Indra and others were standing, "Welcome Devarun, look your brothers have come to meet you." Shesh laughed, he enjoyed taunting those who came to visit Sri Hari.

"The garland given by Rishi Durvasa was Sri itself, it was the wealth, abundance, prosperity, and wellbeing of the entire swarga. But since it was rejected, that Sri has submerged itself in the infinity of Ksheer Sagara." Hari talking about Sri, sounds awkward but that Sagara is me!

Indra was first to interrupt, "Narayan, it is a request. Please ask Varuna dev to give back all he took in."

"Oh, right? I am not bound by the command of a crownless king. Mind your tone with me Purandara, your simhasana has sunk somewhere deep."

Agni was next, "Stop being so difficult!"

I sighed, angry I had to declare- "Go churn me then, churn out the entire ocean and get it back yourself! I will show you real difficulty."

Narayana looked disappointed, Shesh laughed louder "You, devas hiss better than me." This was enough mockery.

"Amrit, do you devas know what Amrit is?" Narayan wasn't looking at us. But naturally the answer came from the Ashwins

"Yes, Amrit is a divine potion, the nectar of immortality. Even a drop of it will liberate the drinker from the cycle of life and birth, eternalising them in their present form." Nasatya recounted a few qualities of Amrit from its taste to colour, things he had learnt from different rishis.

Dasra interrupted, "Amrit is so rare, it is almost mythical. Not even Rishi Kashyap was sure about how it is obtained." This whole conversation made me nauseous to the core, "Why are we talking about Amrit? I feel unwell."

"You are one of us and its catching up to you, this is what weakness feels like when I am not fed with mantras." Agni didn't miss the opportunity to show his disdain, I cant blame him for being frustrated, he was impacted the most.

Vishnu who till now was on his back, laying and looking up into the abyss, tossed around to face us all. Folding his elbow, he rested his head on the palm, this time he was staring at me.

"I would cry now!" didn't mean to say it out loud, now both Agni and Shesh would use this against me in the future.

"Save your tears for when they will start churning you." Shesh commented and I snapped, "If I don't allow you to float, you would drown. I respect you only because of Narayan."

"No, Varuna. Shesh is right, you devas must do Samudra Manthan now. The churning of the cosmic ocean is what will bring back everything you lost. Most importantly, Amrit. There is the element of immortality in Ksheer Sagara. Go churn the ocean and you will receive that nectar of divinity."

Vishnu spoke with ease but to me it all sounded impossible. "Why must I put up with all this Narayan?" I felt even more nauseous than before.

"Indra is not the only deva who has become arrogant. And you, Varuna are not aware yet but within you there are fourteen gems, it is about time they are released." Vishnu had indirectly called me arrogant but what are these gems? Feeling nauseous, I sat cross legged and silenced myself.

29.

Devesha

"Churning this Ksheer Sagara? We have never even seen its expanse!" I exclaimed but the thought of finding Amrit was thrilling enough for me to try.

Narayan wouldn't joke at serious times like this, and we have no other option. "You haven't. The cosmic ocean is always expanding, at a pace faster than your lightening Devendra. Only the trimurti is capable of measuring it." Shesh hissed.

In the last millennial or so, this Naga has never passed an opportunity of putting us down. Maybe because, he bows only to Vishnu.

"But we cannot do this impossible task alone, look at us we are weak." I lamented knowing it may sound like a pathetic excuse, but this is our reality.

"Make some efforts, go align with the asuras. Raja Bali, the king of Daitya Clan is a devotee of mine. Go make a truce." Saying this Narayan went back to his yoga-nidra. The sleep where he one is awake.

Pride? That stupid pride of mine is making me walk to the realm of Daityas. I am leaving for the palace of Bali, my greatest rival along with Guru Brihaspati all because of this pride.

30.

Svarbhanu

Shores of Ksheer Sagara were camped by the armies of devas and daityas. For the first time, we appeared richer, better, and more powerful.

Yet these devas who have lost their everything walk with so much pride around our men, if only once could I swallow their arrogance, I would do so in a heartbeat.

The last I saw them was when I was eight, they had come attacking us. That Surya there killed my father Viprachitti, and that Indra killed Anuhlada. My relatives died at their hands, back when they came clad in gold, silver and weapons.

I am satisfied watching them stoop so low that they came asking Bali for help. Our king Bali has only accepted this fate for he wish to serve Vishnu all the time, but me?

I am Svarbhanu the son of Simhika and Viprachitti, to eternity and beyond I will serve daityas as their army chief and stand against devas.

Bali is a great leader but a timid man, and being our king, he shouldn't be in front lines anyway. I am the diplomat, chief of army. I am going to move forward and have a word with those so-called gods.

"I want one of you devas to come out as representative and coordinate with me." I told Agni who if I remember correct is the mouth and voice of gods, but he is too annoying.

"Here come deal with me, pretty boy." Voice of a man, but when I look into the direction of the speaker, it is just a young boy. Younger than me.

"Who are you? A deva?" I tried confirming as the boy walked towards me, he is a bit shorter but has the built of a warrior. "Yes I am. Call me Mangal, the son of Bhoomi devi."

"Whoever you maybe Mangal or Amangal, this is not a child's playground. Leave and send for an adult." Harsh, I commanded him in the harshest tone possible and so why am I being choked right now?

This young man was fast enough to tackle, choke and put me in a lock. A lethal technique like this could have killed a minor monster but unfortunately for him, I can lift myself enough to throw him on the ground. "So you are a prodigy of war? Good because me too." Putting all my body weight of him was enough to make him gasp, he has gotten weaker too.

"I came from the heat of Shiva's tandav, you fool!" Understandable why he still has me in a lock. I clicked my fingers, gesturing him to release me.

"I would play with you some other time, kid. But I need to sort important matters. I am the Daitya

Senapati. The chief of Asuri armies." Trying to walk past this kid is annoying, he is blocking my way.

"Let sort out the important matters then, general to general. Mangal, the chief commander of divya armies and forces. Kartikey and I are toe to toe in combat." He pumped his chest, don't know whether I should feel intimidated or laugh but yes, he would make a great frenemy.

"Have you seen the Ksheer Sagara? What will churn it with?" asking the real question, the boy pointed at Garuda, the vahana of Vishnu had brought an entire mountain, carried on his back.

"That is Mandaranchal parvat, it will become the churning rod, or you know what goes as the stick? I have never churned anything in life before so don't mind me being ignorant about the technicalities." Mangal is humouring me, this is how most warriors show signs of friendship.

"Very well and do you know we need a rope to churn? A rope big enough to wrap around that mountain and for us to hold." I believe I sound serious then why do I feel a lick behind my back.

Its Shesh Naag, partly submerged in water who had been spying on us. I turned around, his tongue gave me an ick. Mangal laughed, what a field day.

"My brother Vasuki would serve as the rope, Shiva's grace." Shesh remarked. "Why not you?" Mangal asked. "This ocean itself is Naag Laxmi, my wife. I would anything but churn her." He answered.

"Now what is a Laxmi?" I inquired feeling awkward, "You will see that yourself Svarbhanu. Afterall there is Naga in you." Swear, Shesh is the most confusing entity in existence, he is more mysterious than Vishnu at times.

Vasuki is massive, how does Shiva even wear him as a garland is beyond me. Despite his strength and efforts, Mandaranchal Parvat kept sinking in the water. I think that water god is Varuna, he looks exhausted. "I am too weak to keep this heavy mountain afloat, the fishes I am breeding will die. They are extremely dear to me, lord Vishnu." He cries to Vishnu, and I can tell its not his first time doing so. I wonder how much of Ksheer Sagara is just made of his tears.

Now this is such a once in a lifetime moment for both of us Daityas and Devas alike because what we just witnessed was Vishnu leaving behind his chakra, gada and lotus to take the form of a tortoise.

The sages who were looking at us from afar are bowing down to this amphibian, "Koorma Narayan!" they praise him. So, Vishnu took the avatar of a massive tortoise for what?

I looked to my sides, others were equally confused till we witnessed the tortoise, submerging itself deep within the water. He is balancing that heavy mountain on his shell, does he not care about his back? I couldn't hold back my wonder, that looks like real power though compulsively I laughed.

"What is next Vishnu, will you balance a mountain on your fingers? Is this really necessary when you can just perform simple miracles like making Mandara unsinkable, but must you take dramatic avatars?" Confidence, that's what I feel as I joke about the devas and their master Vishnu.

My own superior, Bali looks hurt and stares at me in disbelief. Mangal punched me on the back and told me to align my people instead.

The mountain, our churning rod is upright in the middle of the ocean, Vasuki the giant serpent has wrapped itself around it like a rope with two ends, its tail, and head while the body has coiled around the mount which is supported by a tortoise that is also Vishnu. If in future I ever had children, this legend would be the most fun but difficult to explain.

The daityas stand in a line behind me, Bali is the one who is at front. Cleverly Vishnu has again tricked us into holding the side of snake with his head. It is difficult standing here, this snake fumes. We are literally standing towards the deeper side while those trickster gods are on the shallow end of water.

Never mind, I am doing this all for Amrit because I am tired of Shukracharya holding sole authority over Mrit Sanjeevani.

We started churning the ocean, we did it for months what actually did hurt me was that Mahadeva and Brahma stood at the side of the gods, churning with their end of rope, snake, whatever.

But I cannot blame them, the devas look so weak almost like mortal humans. They disgust me.

We churned for months, and nothing happened, except that the scales of Vasuki rubbed against the trees on the mountain Mandara. The forest there, caught fire but Agni is too weak to order the flames and Vayu too weak to control the smoke that is making Vasuki cry.

This serpent, he is crying not tears but poison. The ocean is poisoned, Varuna has fallen unconscious. Vishnu remains in there, "Get out this is Halahal!" I screamed at the tortoise as we all evacuated to the shores, but all ever happened was Shesh who smirked at me. Snakes these days!

"Halahal is the deadliest poison to ever exist." Bali commented, Indra looked crestfallen until Mahadeva stepped forward, the ocean that appeared black with venom was down in Shiva's throat.

He gulped down Halahal! All for what? Because these devas were praying and crying? I know Shiva wouldn't die but look at him sweating.

"Indra, he is doing this for you and your kind. I promise Shiva deserves not an ounce of this pain." I shouted at the other side.

Indra who was kneeling with his hands joint muttered something about "O greatest, Devadi-deva Mahadeva. It is not just the venom you swallow but our pride as well. I am humbled to my very core."

In a span of some time, I had witnessed Vishnu becoming a tortoise, Shiva drinking Halahal but Indra being humble is the most incredible sight. Who knew this date would come. Shiva looked like he wouldn't be able to handle that venom.

Till I saw Mahakali who came running and putting her hands on his throat. She choked him, she stopped the poison of Shiva in the throat itself.

 It is blue, his throat is blue, "Hara-Hara Neelkanth!" The Rishis exclaimed again, such occasions would make devas shower flower from above, but they stand too below Shiva. Vishnu is underwater and the devas aren't above him either. What exactly makes these gods so different than us? Destiny or power?

"Mahakali is my Aradhya, my adhisthatri devi." I repeated to myself. "What if you choke on Amrit the way Shiva choked on Halahal?" Mangal interrupted my sweet thoughts.

"Try funny things with me boy? I can eclipse entire galaxies at once!" I shooed him off.

31.

Ratnas

The devas and asuras churned the ocean for months, one night in the month of Falgun there emerged a man with silvery aura from the ocean. His flesh so white, so paled in comparison and his brilliance not less than the sun. Surya dev who was burning with heat but had dimmed due to weakness felt relief upon the sight of this man.

The devas rejoiced, the darkness of the sky was dispelled at his sight. The moon god was born for the third time finally coming out to the real world.

"Who are you?" Surya asked his eyes closed in a sweet melody, he hasn't felt this cool or calmed ever. "I am the son of Atri and Anusuya, raised on the nectars of Varuna. My name is Chandra." The man proclaimed walking out to the shore.

He stood in the middle of both sides, Shukracharya called out to him. "Your father Atri and my father Bhrigu have a brotherly bond and such a bond is what I share with you Chandra. The devas are weak, join our side and be a daitya."

"Come here Chandra, you are to the night what Surya is to the day. Be of service, help dispel the dark and bring illumination to the world. I will give you the title of a deva, Oh Atreya! Come join us, we are the favoured sons of Kashyap." Devendra interjected.

Chandra tilted his face, giving half a smile. He walked straight to Shiva, touching the blue throat. The sweat was cooled off, the moon god had a soothing energy.

He fell at the feet of Shiva, "I have heard from Varuna that my father Atri is a devotee of yours. Never understood why it was. But today you drank the very poison which suffocated me in there, Mahadeva you saved me. Let me serve you forever, I choose whatever side you allow me to."

Shiva smiled, "maybe in some future you and I will be even closer but today go join the ranks of devas. You wanted to touch the sunshine? There stands Surya and he needs your healing more than I do."

Chandra happily hopped to the devas, but with Surya his interactions weren't the most pleasant. Varuna nudged the sun god, "Look I think he will be a friend to you, same way Agni is mine." Agni giving a sarcastic laugh engaged in a playful banter till Indra made them churn the ocean again. Chandra was the first Ratna that Varuna released.

Soon after some time, there came out a cow from the ocean. Extraordinarily beautiful this was Kamdhenu, also named Surabhi. This cow had the power to grant any wish and nourish multiple realms at once, but Brahma claimed it and handed over to the rishis.

There came Ucchaishrahva, a seven headed horses that flew at the speed of Vayu. Revanta being the chief of all horses, allowed Raja Bali to have this horse. To balance the scale with Asuras.

The last animal to emerge from the cosmic ocean was Airavat. Indra was overjoyed looking at his companion who had come back, seven trunks and four tusks carved of gold, can a creature more majestic exist anywhere? Indra would say no. Devendra claimed his friend, no one objected because he had smiled for the first time in forever.

Now that Airavat helped Devas in churning the ocean, the process became faster. And so from the ocean had emerged the literal gem, Kaustubh. But the radiations of this gem were too much to bear, it blinded even the sun and moon ultimately Vishnu wore it on the suggestion of Shesh.

Then during the Samudra Manthan, had emerged the tree that could manifest the dreams of anyone, Kalpvruksh. This has the power to make imagination come to life. Indra claimed it for his wife, said the tree deserved to be in gardens of Amravati.

Then was born from the ocean, the divine nymph Rambha. Urvashi devi, the head of Apsaras invited her, and Rambha followed before any man could claim her.

The churning had brought the devas and daityas to the month of Kartik and then emerged with the brilliance of millions of Kaustubh Mani, the queen mother, the devi of universe, a manifestation of Adiparashakti. One of the panch-prakritis. Her skin is made of gold, the flick of her fabric produced gems of all kinds, she was beautiful more than any other devi or apsara that had ever existed. This was Sri who carried a pot of gold in her hand.

Bhoomi bowed to her, Sri Devi and Bhoo Devi were ultimately one. Prakriti worshipping herself is the crux of existence after all.

The appearance of Laxmi, the woman who came holding a pot of gold restored all wealth and abundance of Swarga. Looking at her made the crowns and jewellery of devas reappeared, they all bowed down to her. "We are not foolish enough to claim you mother divine, just requesting you to bless us forever with your grace!" That's all the devas said as Laxmi handed over the key to all treasures of the world to Shesh, "Let Nagas protect all the wealth." She commanded and looked at Kubera.

"Serve me, Deva Kubera. Become the authority that grants, manages, and spends this wealth that comes from me." Kubera whose purpose was being an accountant to devas was rejoiced knowing he would serve Laxmi so closely.

He was tearing up, "Mother divine. I request you to not come to Swarga or not go to the other realms either. Look at us, you provide plenty, but greed is a sin. Anything but to disrespect your dignity."

Laxmi smiled. Looking at all those present, she asked "And so where shall I stay because I cannot be claimed by the devas or the daityas?" Shesh crawled up to her feet, she petted his head gently.

"My swami is a lonely man" He teased making Laxmi look at the ocean, Koorma was there. Vishnu remained there as a tortoise but being omnipresent, he now showed his form.

Skin as blue as deep ocean complemented the golden hues of Laxmi's complexion. "You nourish the three worlds that I protect at all times. You are the wealth of all kinds, without you no realm can survive. I am a poor man, I have nothing much to offer."

He handed over a lotus in full bloom to the devi, "If you love lotuses, my abode has plenty of these. Become the Swamini of Vaikunth and I, marry me, Laxmi. I have been waiting for you since forever."

No participant of Samudra Manthan expected to witness the wedding of Sri and Hari to take place in front of their eyes. Rishi Bhrigu acted as the father of Laxmi and Shukra bowed to her, claiming now they were siblings in relation.

Chandra came rushing too, "We both emerged from this ocean, you are a sister to me as well. But you are the Maa to the three worlds." He felt a bit half hearted till Laxmi responded with a "Yes and so that makes Mama. The maternal uncle to the three worlds."

She laughed, young moon god who couldn't grasp the humour took the role of unclehood quite seriously. The other devas knew this younger addition would bring plenty entertainment once back in swargaloka.

The two-side continued to churn the ocean. All of a sudden, the water changed taste and coloured there suddenly fell all the attendees in a state of daze. They were drunk on some ecstasy, the devas and asuras were knocked off their senses.

There came a woman, holding a mysterious pitch in her hand. She laughed looking at the state of all the men, until one of them called out to her.

"You are a mischievous gem of mine, aren't you?" It was Varuna who remained unfazed. "I am Sura, I ruled the element of intoxication. But why are you unfazed." She said walking close to Varuna.

"I am the ocean itself, no amount of your alcohol would dilute me. Also, what kind of name is Sura? It means Madira and I can't even get drunk." The lady looked a bit disheartened.

"Don't look so sad now. I give you the name Varuni. Ocean is lonely and I wonder whether you could cure it if I claimed you?" Varuna who has never put efforts in his words spoke only naturally what he felt.

Soon followed the matrimonial union of Varuna and Varuni, she had removed the intoxication of others and the water god was happier than ever.

The ocean churned some more, a conch named Panchjanya emerged. This shankh was gifted to Vishnu as a symbol of gratitude.

Another divine bow called Sharanga had emerged but being difficult to lift, Vishnu took it with himself.

At last, when all wait was over, there emerged Dhanwantri. Another avatar of Sri Hari that all recognised as Narayan.

His hand had a pitch filled with Amrit. The daityas were quick to grab it and started running away to their world. Vishnu took the form of an alluring woman, Vishwamohini. The feminine avatar of Vishnu could entice the entire universe with her charms. No man could resist the temptation.

The very pious devas trembled with joy at her sight the daityas were no where resistant. Mohini danced, the world danced with her.

With ease she took back in her hands the pot of Amrit. Cleverly she danced and to devas presented the nectar of immortality while to the asuras only sips of water. But who would notice something so meagre at the sight of this woman? Svarbhanu did.

He tied Chandra somewhere in the corner, took his guise impersonating the moon. A fatal mistake was to sit next to Surya who immediately felt his heat rushing back but this Chandra lacked the cooling effect or silvery brilliance.

Surya came back to his senses, reporting his suspicions to Vishnu. Chandra came back and there were two of him now.

"Svarbhanu is to join Surya and Chandra later as Graha oh Narayan, do not kill him." Brahma declared. "It is too late for him to die, he has had a sip of Amrit!" Chandra pointed at the Daitya Warrior, who quickly gulped his portion of immortality but before the liquid could cross his throat.

The Sudarshan Chakra that Vishnu held in his hand had come slicing down Svarbhanu. He was torn to two pieces, his head fell between Sun and Moon and body to the other side of Surya.

He cried in pain, "Neither am I alive nor can I die." He was angry.

"Because of Surya and Chandra, I have become split. My revenge, I will forever eclipse you two time to time and let you wither in the illusion of death. May you two forever struggle in vain against my darkness." Svarbhanu cursed.

Indra took the Amrit with himself, nobody could fight him now. Bali retreated at the order of Vishnu.

Separated parts of Svarbhanu were pitied upon by Vishnu, they worshiped Shiv and Kali and were nursed by Simhika.

The head of Svarbhanu was attached to the body of a snaked, they name this entity Rahu.

The body of Svarbhanu was attached to the head of that same snake, this entity was known as Ketu.

Rahu the north lunar node and Ketu the south lunar node were separated and remained 180 degrees apart. Surya held each to a side of his and stopped spinning, the other celestial bodies, earth (Bhoomi), mars (Mangal), Venus (Shukra), Jupiter (Brihaspati) and Saturn (Shani) along with Moon (Chandra), Yama (Pluto), Uranus (Aruna) and Neptune (Varuna) started revolving around the Sun to keep Rahu and Ketu apart.

Rahu in his animosity never stopped engulfing the two luminaries. He swallowed both Surya and Chandra with so much of passion that these two gods were never proud again and feared the shadow planets forever.

THE BOOK OF SOMA AND SAUMYA

32.

Indrasabha IV

The gods now drowned in luxuries and pleasure more than ever. Swarga has become the happiest realm, all the immortalised gods lived in bliss. The Asuras calmed and lessened their attacks.

Samudra Manthan might have shattered their arrogance, but the power of Amrit still deluded them. Thank to Parameshwara they had the divine guidance of Brihaspati showing them the way but one time as they sat laughing in the sabha.

The devas joked around, gandharvas played the music and apsaras danced as Devendra on his throne engaged playfully with his wife Shachi. Devaguru Brihaspati entered this hall, for a moment he was happy seeing that everyone else was full of joy but disrespect hurts.

The devas who saw their preceptor very well noticed his presence but ignored him, they laughed with each other. Indra who looked at his minister turned his gaze back to his wife.

Brihaspati exasperated and disappointed claimed. "I sacrificed my tapobala and spiritual powers all to champion each of you. I risked the life of my son for the wellbeing of this sabha and collaborated with Shukracharya, my nemesis for the sake of Amrit. Yet this sabha has greatly ignored my presence. You Indra disrespected your guru to be with your wife, I curse your pair, may you take multiple incarnations in the mortal world craving each other's love to only find the pain. And Indra let you be replaced someday." Brihaspati's curse left the royal couple in despair. But Guru himself disappeared in thin air.

Without Brihaspati there were no yajnas. The devas disappoint being immortal felt the loss of power and guidance, they were now threatened again by the asuras. Brahma who had the goodwill of all at heart, advised the gods to find a new preceptor, a purohit who did yajnas.

There was Tvashta who had penanced for so long and from sacrificial fire had emerged Vishwaroopa.

Vishwaroopa was a noble man, a genius who became the priest of gods. Indra was satisfied and so were the others while Brihaspati was gone, his lonely wife Tara had gone to attend a Yajna at Chandraloka.

Chandra had organised a Rajasuiya yajna, the consecration of a king for he was the newly crowned ruler of Chandraloka. Brihaspati couldn't attend but his wife Tara did.

Meanwhile Indra was flabbergasted by how quickly Vishwaroop has changed. He indulged in luxuries and almost threatened to replace Indra himself.

Not knowing what else could be done, following the advice of Vishnu, Vishwaroop was killed at the hands of Indra. "Brahmahatya. Devi I am now an ugly sinner who committed the grave demerit of Brahmahatya." Devendra cried to Indrani.

"Atone for it! I will wait for you." Indrani replied.

Devendra left for the woods alone, engaging in desperate Tapasya to cleanse his soul.

While Chandra and Tara were so infatuated by each other they eloped.

Brihaspati who heard about Indra's atonement finally came back to him. The sin of Brahmahatya cannot be simply cleansed so Guru took it from Indra and divided it into four parts.

First part of the sin was given to trees that manifested in the form of gum. Second part was given to women which became the phenomenon of menstruation. Third was given to earth making some of the land barren and finally fourth was given to water which came in the form of bubbles and foam.

Though the four were granted the boon of becoming forever pure and sacred, more than any man ever.

Meanwhile when Brihaspati returned back, he found his wife Tara to have taken by Chandra.

Both so lost in lust and infatuation of beauty they refused to let each other go.

The yajnas could not have been performed by a priest if he were married and his wife wasn't by the side.

33.

Budha

I was developing in the womb of Tara, this woman who is my biological mother, whose decisions I do not support at all.

My father is youthful, he is too youthful to be a father but yet I am here, his seed that was growing in the womb of another man's wife.

Even Tara devi herself doesn't know that I have been conceived but I am fully conscious and can hear and see through her all that happens.

Finally, now that my great grandfather, Brahma has intervened, both Tara and Chandra are present in Indrasabha. I can smell Amravati and its flowers. I can hear the disappointment of Brihaspati, Indra's voice is so sharp, but my favourite is the warmth of Surya, he is so unlike the cooling nature of my father.

"The Yajnas cannot be performed if Tara is not by my side. And without Yajnas, all you devas are bound to lose to Asuras. Tara is my rightfully wedded wife, what she feels for Chandra is not real love but infatuation and that is it. I and Tara have already born Kacha before, this is unfair." Brihaspati is reasonable but I dislike his temperament.

"Though Tara is older than me but she is so young to be with Guru. We are couple with beauty and love, just let us live. Devendra, you wouldn't be separated from Indrani then why do this to me?" My young, blooded father has never said something I can agree with. I fear that after my birth we wouldn't get along much but let's save this judgement for later.

"Don't compare me and Indrani to any other couple, we have the most loving yet most lawful marriage." Devendra and pride are like Sun and his light, you cannot separate the two.

"I left my husband on my own accord, I didn't feel loved by him at all. He spent all his time here in your court Indra. And never did I feel his affection?" Mother was speaking.

Brihaspati who felt humiliated, changed his form of the old man with shikha to that of a handsome young prince, who would expect that?

"If it is about appearance, then look at me now. My real face, my youth which I had lost serving the devas as their master. Who says I cannot become pretty like Chandra?" Guru is desperate today, rare.

The court made me laugh, I haven't developed a mouth or any form yet. I am voice itself, very sound of it. The sabha is shocked. "Tara did that voice come from your belly?" Guru asked.

Brahma had appeared in the court, I greeted him from the womb itself. He is overjoyed but everyone else is shocked and confused.

"You, Tara are pregnant with a divine child. This mysterious baby is a form of Vishnu but whose seed do you nourish in the womb?" Asking the question, Brahma disappeared.

The sabha erupted in chaos. Both Brihaspati and Chandra argued, I enjoy this. After all I knew it would happen, I caused this fight deliberately, mischief.

Chandra and Brihaspati are both claiming me as theirs, others don't know whose side to take. I think this is enough. I will speak the truth now, that is the purpose of my life to verbalise truth.

"I am Chandraputra, my father is the son of Atri. There is no trace of Devaguru in me." I declared out loud for the sabha to hear.

"You can speak but how? How long have you been there? When do you come out?" My father's reaction was to bombard me with questions, but he doesn't seem as shocked as others. But now I will go quiet because mischief.

"You child who dares speak, you seed of this indecent man who lives in the womb of my wife. You whose existence had disgraced mine, I curse that you shall not have a gender. Nor will you be born a man neither a woman." An enraged guru cursed me but before I could process, father had taken mother and ran off somewhere.

34.

Chandra

"My lover, she is the wife of Brihaspati, but my child is in her womb!" I stood in front of Shukracharya with Tara by my side.

"The devas will declare an attack on you then." Shukra said engaged in reading of some scripture.

"You once said, I was like a brother to you!" I know my words aren't sensible, but I need to protect them somehow. "Leave Chandra, you abducted the wife of some other man and Brihaspati might be an enemy, but he is more like a brother to me than you." Shukra was adamant but so was I.

"Acharya, I have heard so many praises of you! Brihaspati cannot perform Yajnas while Tara is here and my father is a good fighter, isn't it great how vulnerable Indra is at the moment? Both you and Chandra dev are great devotees of Shiva, would you not protect me? I am an unborn child that too a cursed one." The child spoke from Tara's womb again. He is a sweet voice, but his words can wage wars.

"This is no time for your mischief! You startled the Indrasabha, don't start in the ashram of Shukra." I told the child to shut up, don't know whether it is a he or she after the curse but sounds a little masculine to me. How will I ever father an androgynous talkative prankster? I sighed thinking about the child.

"I can hear you sigh. You started it, now handle!" This baby is something else. I laughed, this is a tense moment, but I laughed. "Be born first, we will see who handles who!"

When I turned my attention back to Shukracharya he was as stunned as Tara. "I am impressed by you, child! I see Chandra have already taken up to the paternal instinct of scolding you." Acharya laughed.

Turning back at me, he smiled- "The last time a father and son pair had such a rocky relationship it was Surya and Shani. Needless to say, I have always sided with Shani against Surya. And this time too, I will fight from your side with the Asuri armies. Remember Chandra, I do not condone your actions, I just love this offspring of yours."

"I will stay here after my birth. I don't want to leave your ashram." The child spoke again, "You will go back to Chandraloka." I replied.

"Oh, you should try going back to Chandraloka first!" The baby has an answer to everything.

35.

Taraka-yudh

A war broke out, Shukracharya and his students were fighting from the side of Chandra while Brihaspati and Indra were on the other end along with the devas. The war kept going on for a long time.

Brahma and the unborn child convinced Chandra to give up on this meaningless war. Tara lost her attraction to the moon god, looking at the bloodshed and a devasur sangram being named after her made her fly back to Brihaspati.

Since the purpose of the war ended both armies withdrew. When Tara gave birth to the child, Indra took the custody before Brihaspati. Guru had not much interest in claiming the child anyway.

Surya thought the baby was as beautiful as Chandra, Chandra who they all used to call Soma out of affection. What to call this intelligent child of his? They gave him the name Saumya, both because the gentle qualities and something from his father.

Brihaspati was not the most thrilled about the child but having a baby to play with shifted the mood of devas. "Why not arrange a naamkaran samskara for him?" Indrani suggested, Indra obliged.

During the naming ceremony, Chandra showed his face which he hadn't till now. Rishi Atri followed.

"The child is mine to name and to raise. He belongs to the gotra of Atri not Kashyap or Angiras." He was bitter in words.

"Saumya will make a better deva or perhaps a devi compared to you." Surya commented. "Saumya? That name is not fitting enough." Chandra retorted.

The naming ceremony involved a sacrificial fire, Agni had summoned the presence of trideva for the same. Shiva was first to speak, "Chandra, my beloved, you are the controller of mind and emotions. But this child has the potential to become the ruler of brain and thoughts, thus surpassing you in some way." Narayan held the child in his hands, "He will join you as one of the graha, a planet in your system. And I will become his adhisthatri devta."

Having Vishnu as one's ruling deity was no joke and Chandra understood this well. Brahma at last spoke, "The child is ruler of Buddhi, intellect but most importantly since his conception he showed awareness, such bodh at early age. I name him Budha." Thus was the planet Mercury got his name.

36.

Chandra

Budha has turned into a mischievous toddler, he keeps reaching for my hair and grabbing them. Such disruption while I am in the middle of Aradhana.

"Hold the shringi properly and do the abhishek." Correcting the position of his tiny hands, I instructed him about the way of worshipping Shivalinga. He asks way too many questions but waits for the answer of none.

Finally, there is someone who recognises me as the element of Brahma and tries to test my knowledge.

"Baba, I want a mother." He said the same words he has been speaking since last few months and I have grown tired.

"The moon is pretty, isn't it?" I ask. He pulled my hair tighter. "The stars are prettier. I like those constellations. The one named Rohini is my favourite." He is trying to taunt me.

"Very well, so you know?" I inquire, making him lay down on my lap. "I know everything, you have been seeing the daughter of Daksh Prajapati since past few months." I feel sometimes that this baby grows at a pace faster than he should.

"Hmm... But Prajapati has a condition, I must marry all the nakshatras. His daughters that are the goddesses of various constellations." I answer.

"And that is a good thing. You get 27 of them so you will never get bored." Budh is mischievous, I wish to find a tutor for him but Brihaspati and him cannot stand each other.

"I want a mother! Please! You need a wife too!" He kept nagging and at some point, I agreed.

I married the 27 daughters of Daksha Prajapati. The nakshatra sisters were all beautiful and brilliant. Budh loved Rohini the same way I did but his preference shifted to Jyestha, Ashlesha and Revati who were more maternal to him.

Budha left for Suryaloka as Surya had accepted him as a student and to be fair, he is one of the best teachers you could ever get. My trouble was to ensure this child wasn't over influenced by Shani, Rahu or Ketu, all three of them have a disdain for me.

Rohini and I kept growing closer, the time I spent with other 26 of my wives diminished gradually and so one day my father-in-law called in.

"You love Rohini so much that my other daughters feel no affection from you. Do something about it!" Prajapati ordered, I refused then he cursed me.

"Oh, Chandra may your light diminish slowly as your love did for 26 of my daughters and may your beauty and glow fade out completely."

The curse made me lose all that I had. Rohini suggested that pleasing Mahadeva would be the only way. And so, I went down on earth.

Somnath, the first ever Jyotirlinga was established by me. I performed penance day and night till Shiva appeared. "I cannot reverse the curse, but you will not fade into obscurity. This fullness you shall attain only once a month but be blackened completely for a night, you Chandra must go through sixteen phases every fortnight."

And since the moon had his phases, aligned to wombs of women and waves of ocean.

Following my footsteps perhaps, years after Budha returned home. "I finally have become a man in flesh and body. Narayan blessed me." He said.

After his days of Tapasya, he had attained a form. He looked so much like me but had hints of Tara all over his face. Memories hurt.

37.

Chandravansh

Ikshvaku founder of solar dynasty left the lineage of Sun named Suryavansh on earth. The brother if Ikshvaku, Vaivasvata Manu was childless for a long time until by the divine grace of Mitra and Varuna he was blessed by an offspring.

The blessing of mitravarun should have bore a daughter but due to the stubborn intent of Manu, this child was a son named Sudyumna.

Sudyumna who grew up to be a handsome young prince rode his horses often to explore the forests. One fateful day he entered the sacred grove known as Devadaru.

This grove of enchantments turned Sudyumna's body into that of a woman as immediate effect. He pleaded to the gods and the curse gave him two options. Either transform into a woman forever or interchange his gender from man to woman and woman to man, every month alternatively.

Sudyumna whose purpose of birth was to carry forward the lineage of Surya and Manu chose the latter. But his transformations greatly interested the planet Mercury, Budha.

Budh himself had gone through the phases of gender transformations, he was a eunuch and God of gender fluidity. He approached Ila, the feminine version of Sudyumna and they both resonated with each other.

As a woman Ila would stay with Budha but as a prince, Sudyumna would return to his kingdom in the form of a man.

Ila bore a half human and half godly child with the seed of Budha. This boy was named Pururavas thus started the lunar dynasty.

Pururavas named his lineage after his grandfather which came to be known as Chandravansh.

Later Sudyumna father three sons for the solar dynasty and upon his death took the form of Ila, staying as the consort of Budha.

This story was narrated often to Nahush, a king of Chandravansh who was a noble ruler.

38.

Vajra

Tvashta the one who once fathered Vishwaroop lost his son to the insecurities of Indra and with nothing but pure hatred. He created another son, one equivalent to Indra in almost everything.

Vrutrasura was born and greatly threatened Devendra. To show his dominance, he took the form of a giant dragon blocking the seven rivers. Earth faced draughts like no others. Sapt Sindhus were blocked, the thirsty Aryans called upon Indra for rain, but the rivers remained captured by Vrutra.

Under the guidance of Vishnu, Indra guised in the form of a man went on to befriend him first. Vrutrasura who despite being malicious grew a liking to this man and entrusted him. One day while drunk, Vrutra told Indra the secret of his defeat.

Apparently Vrutra can be killed only with a divine weapon which was too peculiar to be found or crafted. Indra and the devas approached Rishi Dhadhichi and the great sage at once told them the method, sacrificing his life and leaving behind his corpse. Kamdhenu licked the flesh and what was left behind were the bones of Dhadhichi.

With the bones of the rishi who sacrificed himself, thus was crafted the greatest of all divine weapons in existence for the greatest of all divine king, Vajra.

The secret of killing Vrutra lied in this weapon called Vajra, the yielder of it Devaraja Indra.

In a fierce battle between the serpent and the god of lightening, the vajra stuck Vrutra thus freeing the rivers and nourishing the earth.

Indra rained the earth with so much of joy that the season of monsoon became part of the year. The ruler of Shravana month which he dedicated to Mahadeva.

Indra yet again was tainted with the sin of Brahmahatya, all gods together brought waters of holy rivers, bathing and cleansing him. The devas out of adoration and admiration looked at their great king, anointing him as their hero.

Indra was arrogant, he was foolish at times. Indulgent and maybe sinful but he alone is the one capable of ruling all the worlds. Heaven will never receive a king as great as Purandara and the devas knew this for a fact so did all intelligent races.

39.

Shachi

"I am guilty, guiltier than ever!" my husband cried in my arms. "I killed him using a dirty tactic, its not just the grave sin of Brahmahatya but I killed Vrutra posing as his friend first. I betrayed someone who trusted me, I am ashamed to call myself a warrior." This was the third night after his homecoming where he kept crying with guilt.

"Atone" I whispered, he handed his Vajra to me. "Only you as my shakti can wield this weapon, none but you and I" he said, lulling me to sleep.

I woke up not finding him in the room, the day went searching for him in Amravati which was empty, and all devas reported him to be missing.

Days passed, months passed and without him I felt empty. My duty was to first serve my husband and later on this throne. Heaven to me is meaningless without me, my interest in devasabhas vanished.

I spent my days and nights calling Indra, chanting his name and mantras. I worshipped him, I worshipped all the gods to bring him back or just take me to him.

The devas appointed Nahush as a temporary king. That filthy sick man lusted after me. "I have heard you never said NO to Indra? Well, I am Indra now." He declared calling me out in front of everyone.

"Oh Indrani, you belong to Indra. I am Indra, the crown, palace, throne of Purandara all belong to me now and so why shouldn't you become mine?" He said, I left the palace immediately.

Finally, I called upon Indra in so much of distress, that he came flying back. He took me away to a dingy cave away from the world, alone.

"Shachi, stop crying! You know out of all things I left behind, you are all that I missed." He said trying to soothe me down.

"I am a man of sin and filth, I will return only when I become worthy of you again." He kept consoling me, I refused to budge out of his embrace. Talking to him about his replacement and his immoral desire.

"You are the strongest and smartest woman I know, why did you not take over the throne as a rightful queen?" He asked, I was silent. "Go Shachi, you can deal with a minor problem like this."

I didn't go back to palace but did send a message to Nahush. When I first married Indra, he brought my palanquin with him.

If Nahush desires to do the same, he must come on a precession where all devas attend as servants and Nahush be lifted on a palanquin too but let only the saptrishis carry it.

The plan succeeded, Nahush did as I asked him to and while being lifted by the rishis he grew impatient. Kicking the Rishi Agastya who had the quick temper Agni and the same limp in leg as Shani. The angry sage cursed the actual arrogant king.

Nahush turned into a snake and fell on earth, I resumed the throne until one day a peacock came in the garden of Amravati.

"Never leave me alone again!" I kneeled in front of the bird, turning back to his usual form. Devendra laughed, "Oh Shachi. No matter how far apart but we will find each other in heaven or even beyond."

The gods have many other stories some tied closely to the epics of Ramayana and Mahabharata. How much of that is Itehaas and literal history and how much of that is symbolism which encrypts knowledge of philosophy and supernatural, now that I don't not know but all glories be to the devas of swarga.

THANKYOU